ON THE EDGE

MARKUS WERNER was born in Switzerland in 1944. He studied at the University of Zurich, then taught at a school in Schaffhausen until 1990 when he became a freelance writer. His prestigious literary awards include the Jürgen Ponto Stiftung Prize (1984), the Prix Littéraire Lipp (1995), and the SWF Bestenliste Prize in 1997. He has published seven novels, including the bestselling *Zündel's Departure*.

ROBERT E. GOODWIN is a member of the faculty at Skidmore College in Saratoga Springs, NY. He is the author of *The Playworld of Sanskrit Drama* and translator of Rüdiger Safranski's *Romanticism: A German Affair*, forthcoming from Northwestern University Press. He currently lives in upstate New York.

ON THE EDGE

MARKUS WERNER

Translated from the German by
ROBERT E. GOODWIN

Originally published as: "Am Hang" by Markus Werner
Copyright © S. Fischer Verlag GmbH, Frankfurt am Main 2004

Translation copyright © 2012 by Robert E. Goodwin

First published in Great Britain in 2012 by
HAUS PUBLISHING LTD.
70 Cadogan Place, London SW1X 9AH
www.hauspublishing.com

ISBN 978 1 908323 22 4

Typset in Garamond by MacGuru Ltd
info@macguru.org.uk

Printed in Great Britain by CPI Group (UK) Ltd, Croydon, CR0 4YY

I

EVERYTHING'S TURNING. And everything's turning round *him*. It's insane, but I'm even tempted to think that he's sneaking around the house right now – with or without a dagger. Although he's supposed to have left, and I'm just hearing crickets and the distant barking of dogs in the night.

I drive down to Ticino over Pentecost, planning to use the quiet to immerse myself in the history of divorce law, and then this stranger crosses my path, this Loos, and manages to churn me up to such a degree that all my composure is shot. Eva told me the rest over in Cademario today. I drove back here with my head spinning and called the law journal, or rather the editor's private phone since this is Pentecost Sunday, to tell him I can't make the deadline with the article. I told him I had an acute sinus infection, along with a fever, pinching my nose as I spoke. He said he could certainly hear how bad it was.

Yes, it's bad all right. Oh the sinuses are fine, and I have no temperature, but I could certainly describe what's ailing me as a fever. My temples, at any rate, which I press with my fingers to dampen the tumult behind them, are so hot it's as if my thoughts were generating frictional heat as they circle frantically around the same point.

It would be nice to sleep now, shake Loos off, brush Loos's words out of my brain, where they stick like lint. He said to me himself, 'Don't forget to forget, or you'll go mad.' He must know. But he also said, admittedly in another context, that of all the plagues in our time forgetfulness is the most insidious.

All right, I can see that I'm not going to get rid of this man just by commanding myself to stop thinking about him. He'd only become more diffuse and squeeze my consciousness into a rawer state than it's already in. I know the phenomenon from the time Andrea – it was fifteen years ago, when I was twenty – left me behind like a forgotten umbrella. In the meantime I've learned how to stop the machine and proceed methodically with the tangled threads. Go back to the beginning. Carefully undo the knots and snarls. Unravel the yarn, without haste, and at the same time rewind it neatly and tautly on a spool.

Easily said, is it not, my dear Loos? Something you've completely failed to do, in any case, if you've ever even tried it. Have you? Or have you always handled your tangle, your yarn, so – how shall I say – *fantastically* as on the Bellevue terrace?

On the Friday before Pentecost, the congestion at the Gotthard tunnel kept itself within limits, and I made it here a little before six. I opened the water valve, as usual, flicked off the security switch, turned the water heater and the refrigerator on, and took a cold shower. I then disposed of the empty bottles my lawyer colleague and co-owner of the house had left here over Easter. No need for a fire in the fireplace, since it was a mild June evening, so mild that I got back into the car around eight, drove from Agra to Montagnola, and parked in front of the Hotel Bellevue or Bellavista. I was disappointed to see that there was no table free on the terrace, but since I didn't want to sit in the glassed-in annexe, I stood there undecided, hoping to catch sight of diners moving their chairs back from a table. That's when I discovered him. He was sitting alone at a table for four in the left corner of the terrace, so I pulled myself together, went over to him – he was studying the menu – and asked him in Italian if he minded. He looked up for a second and said nothing. I repeated the question in German and, when he nodded absently, sat down across from him at the table.

I noticed, while I waited for a menu, that he looked up from his from time to time and turned his head a little, letting his eyes rest on the hills and slopes on the other side of the valley. His head was a large, strong-boned skull, hairless except for a thick but trimmed half-crown that went from temple to temple, and a just as thick three-day beard flecked with grey. The head appeared heavy, the whole man heavy and massive, but the mass gave no impression of flab; it was all compact. I judged him a good fifty years old. When the waiter brought me the menu, I heard him order his meal with a deep, slightly nasal voice. A carafe filled with white wine was already on the table, and he now reached for his glass and slowly drained it, with his gaze again on the hills. Of me he took no notice at all. As I leafed through the menu, my finger rested on the *filetto di coniglio*, and I started slightly. Up to this moment I had not for an instant thought of Valerie. We had both sat here some while ago eating filet of rabbit, she still full of cheer, I rather taciturn, feeling a knot in my throat, as I rehearsed considerate ways of telling her I wanted to end the relationship.

The sun sank, and, as the lake below began to lose colour, the wine sparkled in the stranger's carafe. 'What a golden yellow,' I heard myself say; 'may I ask what you're drinking?' He turned to me, after a delay, and looked at me as if he were only now aware of my presence. He gave me a look that was not dismissive, not unfriendly, merely surprised. I immediately noticed the shadows under his light grey eyes. They weren't bags from fatigue or tear sacs, but slight discolourations of the skin that I'd only observed before on people of Indian descent. 'Excuse me,' said the stranger, 'what did you ask?' 'I don't mean to bother you,' I said. 'I was asking about the wine you're drinking.' 'It's a white wine,' he said. Although I didn't necessarily take this as a put-on, I felt defensive and said, 'I can see that in any case.' 'Excuse me, what?' he asked. I bit my lips and asked whether he could recommend his wine. He considered this for a moment and then said, 'We always found it congenial.'

I ordered saltimbocca with rice, like my table companion, and a half of white. My companion smoked with his face averted. I didn't exclude the idea that we had only half understood each other, since you could hardly speak of quiet in this place. We were not only surrounded by clatter and the babble of voices, there was the typical drone of occasional planes taking off and landing from the airport down in Agno, and even at this height we could still hear the distant noise of the traffic in the valley as a muffled roar strengthened and reflected by the lake. When my wine came I used the opportunity to break the ice again – I'm an outgoing person and find it unnatural to sit at a table with somebody else in silence – so I lifted my glass and said, 'Your health! My name is Clarin.' He winced, so that the cigarette ash that he had forgotten to tip fell on his napkin. He reached with his left hand for his glass and said, 'Glad to meet you.' But on his part, he seemed to have no intention of introducing himself. I saw that he wore two rings on his finger, plain wedding rings, and inferred that he was probably a widower. A clue anyway, I said to myself, in case he doesn't otherwise reveal himself. Most people you can classify in a basic way after fifteen minutes, even if they don't say a word; you can at least rank them as sympathetic or unsympathetic. But with him I couldn't determine even this much. I only knew that he interested me. He made me think of Valerie, her opaqueness, which fascinated me at the beginning, but ended up putting me off. 'How do you find it?' he suddenly asked me. Now I was the one who winced. 'The wine?' I asked. 'No,' he said, 'the prospect, the view.' I said I found it beautiful, especially just then, with the sun just gone down and the panorama opposite consisting only of dark blue tones – and besides I had been acquainted with the landscape for years. He nodded with satisfaction and said, '"Acquainted with it for years" – that's an interesting way of putting it. And those blue tones: might you be a painter?' 'No,' I said, 'I'm a jurist, a lawyer, and you?' 'So,' he said with a slight and, I thought, almost contemptuous inflection. My question to him he ignored, but he could well not have heard it, since the waiter had just brought the food.

Before reaching for knife and fork he bent his head and closed his eyes for a few seconds. Of course, I thought, he's a priest, black pants, black jacket. I should have thought of that earlier. He ate slowly, self-preoccupied, but in spite of that I spoke to him again. 'Today while I was stalled in traffic on the Gotthard, it suddenly dawned on me that I've forgotten the meaning of Pentecost, I mean what it celebrates.

Isn't that embarrassing?' He stopped chewing, swallowed, and said, 'I'm always inordinately pleased to hear the traffic reports, but as to Pentecost, it's the licking tongues of flame.' He continued eating, while I paused, remembering that you have to humour crackpots, and asked, 'Where do they lick, then, these flames?' He took his time, poured himself another glass of wine, drank. 'They lick,' he said, 'over the heads of the twelve apostles, and they symbolise the Holy Spirit, who came over and into them fifty days after Easter, literally to raise their spirits for the effectiveness of their mission.' 'Bravo!' I said. 'One might take you for a theologian.' 'So,' he said, 'you've revised your notion that I'm a crackpot.' I was startled and asked him where he had got that idea. 'Eyes are very revealing, Mr Clarin,' he said. 'Sometimes I can even hear a sentence spoken only in the mind. It takes no effort at all, as long as eye and ear have not been trained to avoid lingering.' I was surprised that he had been able to remember my name and pronounce it with the right accent, on the second syllable. I thought it was finally time to learn his. He acted as if he had to reflect when I asked him, and then said, 'Loos, Loos with two *o*'s, but we're sitting high and dry. Are you with me if I order another?'

The table was cleared, the merlot bianco brought, and an alphorn sounded in the distance. Loos listened with a rather pained expression. I asked if it irritated him. In principle, he said, he had nothing against the alphorn as such, it was, so to speak, the ideal instrument for dwarfs, and besides it was far from him to criticise a bumbling ardour; the only thing that bothered him was the introduction of the alphorn into Ticino. 'The wonderful local glockenspiels are enough for me too,' I said. 'You like them too? – I'm delighted,' he said. 'They're one reason I come here. You won't find more melancholy sounds anywhere.' I asked whether he was staying in the Bellevue. 'Yes,' he said and looked up at the façade. 'Way up there on the left, that's my watchtower. From there I can see across, over the trees, over the valley. And you? Are you staying here too?' 'In Agra,' I said. 'I have a small vacation house in Agra.' 'To recuperate there over Pentecost from your stresses and strains as a lawyer?' 'Not really,' I said. 'It's a work vacation. I want to write here undisturbed.' 'A nice hobby,' said Loos. 'Is it going to be a novel?' 'You misunderstand,' I said. 'It's professional work, a legal-historical article for a law journal on the subject of marriage law, divorce law primarily. I do a lot of work with that in my practice, and I've developed a historical interest in the subject.'

'Now the lights are going on over there,' Loos said. I cleaned my spectacles in disgruntled silence. 'Retrospection is always good,' he said. 'Really. Retrospection is important, though not in keeping with the time, but I hardly open my mouth any more to address the present time, because the present time always cuts me short. And even though I only say to it, "You have a past, and I measure you first by that past and second by those few dreams that I haven't been able to banish," it has already taken umbrage and refuses to listen.' 'I'm not sure I really understand you,' I said. 'You mean that people who devote themselves to the present, who go with the time, as one says, react with irritation to criticism?' 'Yes, more or less,' said Loos, 'but it's still too early.' 'Too early for what?' 'Too early to talk about the Zeitgeist and the brood that snuggle up to it. I need a few more glasses first. You can measure the level of my intimidation both by that need and by the fact that I haven't knitted my brow even once since we've been sitting on this lovely terrace, though during this time a mobile phone has peeped or chirped no less than fourteen times by my count, and so on. But to get back to the point, it must be disillusioning for you to be constantly confronted with divorce cases. Doesn't it tempt you to regard marriage as impracticable?' *Tempt*, I said, wasn't the word; the right one was *convince*. I was positively compelled by the constant torment I saw couples in to regard marriage as a mistake, or at least a simple overburdening of human nature, which seems too wayward to allow itself to be permanently tamed or to be able to accept the few rules that might make marriage possible, if they were followed. It defied all description, I said, what couples did to each other once they got divorced, whether by continuing to act the same way they had acted during the marriage or by denigrating their former happiness. But the craziest thing was that people couldn't keep from marrying, despite the fact one of every two marriages already ended in divorce, and it was even crazier that more than twenty per cent of divorced couples get remarried.

Loos, who had listened so attentively that I would gladly have gone into more detail, interrupted me and said, 'You're a bachelor, then.' 'A confirmed one, as you have possibly deduced.' 'Then *your* human nature is not overburdened; I'm glad of that,' he said. And while I was still considering whether he meant that seriously or sarcastically, he said quietly, 'For me it was home.' I tried to catch his eye, but he was looking across the valley. 'What was?' I asked. 'Marriage,' he said. 'Was?' He nodded. 'Are you – widowed?' He drank. 'You know,' he said, 'I'm not unfamiliar with your statistics. I even know that there are two million dust mites rioting in every marriage bed, and I've learned from an even more disturbing study that after six years of marriage German couples speak to each other for an average of nine minutes a day, and Americans four point two.' 'Exactly, exactly,' I said. 'And now I ask you,' he continued, 'whether this finding permits conclusions about human nature or perhaps rather about the nightly TV ritual, among other things.' 'Both, presumably,' I said, 'for if we accept that couples' increasing reticence depends on increasing TV consumption, the question remains why the TV screen is preferred to an hour of conversation. It isn't true – I hear this often as a lawyer – that people don't talk because they're watching television. No, people watch television because there's nothing more to talk about, at least nothing new or interesting. "It's gone dead" – that's the expression I hear most often; and from that I conclude that human nature craves diversion and colour, and can't really get used to habit.' 'You're all too right to be right,' Loos said, 'and, as I said, my experience is different. Your health!'

'Your health, Mr Loos. I didn't mean to offend you. I know, of course, that there are happy marriages.' 'That doesn't interest me,' he said. 'Sorry, I thought that was our subject.' 'It's really curious,' he said, 'the more the Zeitgeist seeps into our souls and dictates our behaviour, the more stubbornly we appeal to human nature. One might think it was a question of nostalgia – since our nature has so long been stunted – rather than a trick to absolve ourselves of guilt: everything genetically determined, everything excused: "Just look at the chimps, they don't get married, they rove and stay mobile.'"

Loos seemed not to notice that, while he was speaking, two flies were copulating on his scalp. He's unusually worked-up, I concluded, I need to soften the tone. He probably found it hard to believe, I said, that I would have become a jurist, if I called accountability, and therefore guilt, into question. But it was simply that I couldn't seal myself off from scientific knowledge, which showed beyond doubt how little scope for freedom our genes leave us. Loos drank and shook his head, and said that twenty-five years ago science had proven, also without doubt, that even dementia was possibly learned and that the individual was formed, normed, and, as a rule, deformed, to the very marrow, by influences from the environment. I said that science was not in the habit of standing still, but that I admitted the truth might lie in the middle. He begged me to spare him the middle, he was too old for it. In any case, he had no intention, he said, of nodding politely to both sides to the end of his days, and he had just now thought of an addendum to what we had touched on earlier in our discussion. He asked how it happened that people sat happily in front of the TV, evening after evening, craving the same thing over and over, their series, for example, their quiz shows and so forth, whose popularity obviously consisted in their constant and unremitting repetition of the familiar. How did it happen that hundreds of thousands of people were fixated on a moderator's or talk show host's moustache and that a howl would sweep through the nation when he suddenly appeared without it? How could it be explained that the desire for the most inane uniformity was felt only in front of the television screen and not in the rest of everyday married life? But no sooner did people get up from their chairs than they started thinking about divorce, just because their partners were brushing their teeth and gargling the same way they did the day before. 'What, Mr Clarin, is our nature really after?'

It didn't seem an easy question to me. I said I was suddenly getting a little cool and just wanted to get my jacket from the car, if he would excuse me for a moment. '"To be free of hunger, thirst and cold,"' Loos said, 'on that we are united. Perhaps something further will occur to you.' He looked at me expectantly when I got back and asked, 'And?' I saw myself as a high school student standing at the blackboard, with the eyes of the class on me, and reacting blankly to the teacher's expectant 'And?' Loos asked if I was all right. Yes, I said, but for a few seconds I felt the way I used to when I was being quizzed by a teacher. 'For God's sake,' cried Loos, 'I'm sorry. Nothing is further from my mind than playing the teacher. I asked out of genuine curiosity. You're a young man with different horizons, different conceptions, while I'm a senior citizen prone to rigidity. I have to make a hellish effort to stay flexible.' He stopped. I was considering what I would answer. 'But in my heart of hearts,' he said in a muted voice, 'I am not open-minded – that is the curse of fidelity.' He had just given me my cue, I said. It was quite possible that our nature required both: the solid and the liquid, repetition and change, structure and freedom. Loos said he would endorse my diagnosis, if it didn't sound so convincing. I was quite aware, I said, that everything was more complex. That too stood to reason, he said.

The waiter changed the ashtrays. We could hear thundering in the distance. I raised my head and saw only stars. Loos's stubbed-out cigarette still glowed, a ribbon of smoke rose up from it, and I thought again of Valerie who never succeeded in stubbing out a cigarette on the first try. He could be deceiving himself, Loos now said, but he thought he had seen from the way I cleaned my spectacles how much I took my place in life for granted – was his suspicion correct? He really *is* a bit of a crackpot, I thought and asked in return if he could be a little more specific about the way I cleaned my spectacles. 'Just taking it for granted,' he said, 'completely by the by – no anxiety that they might fall out of your hands and break.' 'From that anxiety I am indeed free,'

I said, 'and if I weren't, it would be all the more likely that what I feared would occur. It's like stumbling. A person who goes along in constant fear of stumbling is guaranteed to stumble. In short, it's completely foreign to me to make things in life more difficult than they have to be. So to that extent you are not deceived.' That sounded quite plausible, Loos said, and yet he was convinced that people stumbled far more often from lack of attentiveness than from anxiety about stumbling. I begged him not to take me so literally about the stumbling – I had simply meant that people could, as it were, worry an accident into happening, which didn't mean at all that there wasn't the other kind of accident that strikes us like a bolt out of the blue.

Loos rummaged in his jacket pocket and pulled out a small black spiral notebook and a small black pencil. He leafed through it, obviously looking for a blank page. Although he tried to shield it a little with his left hand, I saw that it was full of jottings and tiny sketches. He noted something down – it couldn't have been more than a word – and stuck the notebook back in his pocket. Then he said more to himself than to me, 'There's something in that. I was always anxious about losing my wife, and one day I did lose her. And yet despite that, it was a bolt out of the blue.' 'I'm sorry,' I said. He nodded and drank. After a while I asked when she had died. For the moment, he said, he couldn't talk about it, perhaps later. I should talk a bit about myself, for example about whether bachelorhood was to my liking. I said that as already mentioned I was not a bachelor against my will; my status was both willed and agreeable. It was unthinkable for me to give up independence and self-determination, and hardly necessary, since a person without ties could enjoy the pleasures that life has to offer with much more abandon. The reproach that I was afraid of accepting responsibility I had to reject, if only because those making it were always those who were groaning about the burden of responsibility themselves. 'You're not standing before a court here,' Loos said, 'but go on with your account.' Naturally it sometimes came to tears, I said, if I was honest and suggested to a woman who expected more from me than I was capable of investing that we should separate. But such tears were trifles compared with any kind of marriage-misery. In most cases the pain of the break-up was very quickly over. For example, I was remembering today, on this terrace, a girlfriend I was here with for the last time some while back, and for her too there was no world collapse. And that was the way it usually went. Looser relationships prevented tragedies and in addition offered protection from the mournful fate that seldom spared traditional couples. Here I paused briefly to take a sip of wine, and Loos, who was following closely, asked, 'Namely?' 'I've already hinted at it,' I said. 'I'm talking about the marriage ladder, where you climb down from desire to liking, to pleasant habit, to list-lessness, all the way to aversion and possibly hatred. Then comes the hour of professional or non-professional counsellors, and maybe a see-through negligee or a desperate tanga provides a few last sparks, and then it's the lawyer's turn.'

'Why so heated?' Loos asked. 'No one's claiming the opposite. Marriage suits only a few, it overburdens the majority. I'd only like to ask you not to use the word "invest" when you talk about relation-ships, because look,' – here Loos pulled up the sleeve of his jacket and showed me his forearm, on which I saw a few red spots – 'look, I'm allergic.' I laughed at what I took for a joke, but he remained serious and said that he often liked to read personal ads, because he wanted to stay abreast of the times, and wherever else the times reflected their character they certainly did so in the personals. There he had recently come upon the ad of a thirty-year-old male who described himself as 'compatible with everyone' and then under the 'Requirements Profile' enumerated the necessary characteristics of his desired partner, when suddenly he, Loos, became aware of red bumps erupting on his left forearm. I said, half laughing, half disgruntled, that I would try to take his allergy into consideration, even if it went against my grain to weigh every word. 'Every word, no, not every word,' said Loos, 'and actually I'm envious of you for being a cautious investor where your feelings are concerned. That way your losses stay manageable. On the other hand, of course, we have to consider that the lower risk minimises the prospects of gain. What does a savings account yield? Enough for a few trips from Zurich to Oerlikon. Whereas a more adventurous outlay of capital might bring such a windfall that you could sail around the world, don't you think?' 'Tease me all you like,' I said, 'I'm not very sensitive. Besides, I understand what you mean. But your analogy has a hitch and takes me too literally. We don't have the power of disposal over our feelings – I too realise that. It isn't fair to use it against me that I haven't yet experienced the so-called great love. Do I have to renounce excursions to the countryside simply because for the time being no opportunity of sailing round the world seems to beckon?' 'Ah, see?' Loos said. 'Before this, virtually everything you said has sounded very premeditated, as if you had everything under control; now you sound more human. But it's not my place in any case to judge the way you live your life. Nor will I ask whether it would remain just a matter of a few tears if a woman loved you blindly and compulsively, whether your – how should I put it? – "tragedy prevention" measures would still work then. But as I said – and you can believe me in this – there's also a little envy speaking out of me: something in me feels sympathetic to the fleeting Eros, the playful form of love. Only I hardly know it, I'm too heavy for it, and not even now that I'm alone and apparently free, do I feel myself capable of it. When I asked you whether bachelorhood was to your liking, I wanted to hear you praise it, because it's not to *my* liking, because I can see little of its positive side. What I do see, by contrast, to mention just one or two things, is this: How mournful a toothbrush looks standing in the glass by itself, and how often I lack a reason to fall asleep at night, an embrace for instance, a kiss, an argument for all I care, in short anything that would allow me to turn to the wall and settle, fractious or contented, into the foetal posture of sleep – I'm sorry! I'm feeling the wine. I think it's time.' 'You're leaving already?' 'Time for the Zeitgeist,' Loos said, 'but first I have to take a quick trip to my room, I'll be right back.' While he was still getting up

I said that we had certainly already said one or two things about the Zeitgeist. 'Too tame,' Loos murmured, went a few steps – he walked like a bear – stopped, turned around, and called out so loudly that the other guests went quiet, 'Too tame!'

I too felt the wine, but no fatigue at all. Something isn't right about this man, I thought. He's hardly a pleasant companion, and yet when I thought he was leaving I was prepared to hold him back with claws if necessary. What in the world is going on?

'So,' he said, 'here I am again. Have you too ever noticed that as soon as we step into a bathroom in a hotel room we're greeted by the so-called hygiene bag for "women's sanitary products"?' 'Does that bother you?' I asked. 'No,' he said, 'it just intimidates me. But what really gets on my nerves is that when I'm back in the room and turn the TV on for a second, the first thing I see is radiant women in the bloom of life romping blissfully on the beach thanks to these women's sanitary products.' 'Maybe you should take such commercials with more humour.' 'I've tried; it doesn't work, Mr Clarin. But actually I was thinking, up there in the bathroom, about the marriage ladder you told me about, that for you leads from heaven to hell. But a really compelling relationship – I have twelve years experience – presents a different picture. Wait, I'll sketch it for you.' While he brought out his notebook and pencil I asked if he did artwork. 'Only privately,' he said gruffly and with a few deft strokes drew a ladder whose foot was surrounded by flames, around which two horned devils danced, and whose upper end leaned against a cloud where an angel sat. 'It may be,' said Loos, 'that a couple begin together on the top rung right under the seventh heaven. Infatuation, passion, drive. It may be too that they end on the lowest rung just above hell-fire. Aversion, disgust, hatred. I say "may be," since not even that is certain. But your model seems wrong to me above all in the assumption that couples climb down at the same time and with the same feelings, some leisurely, others in a race, but always shoulder to shoulder. It's not so mechanical – I almost said *harmonious* – on my ladder: it's a lively bustle, not an orderly line of one-way traffic bound for hell. Both partners climb up and down, crossing each other in the process, and perhaps sit on the same rung now and then – if possible on a high one, where they experience trust and feelings of closeness – and this enables them to move apart again and wave to each other across the different rungs. If they're lucky, the dynamic process on the ladder lasts all their lives, and in an extreme case they'd even make the discovery that hatred doesn't have to kill – on the contrary. – What about some cheese? Are you with me?'

'Gladly,' I said, 'but what do you mean "on the contrary"?' Loos clapped his notebook shut without answering. Then he flipped it open again to a very simply drawn figure and asked, 'What is that?' 'It looks like an eight,' I said, 'but it could be an hour-glass.' He nodded. 'It's my wife's figure,' he said and called for the waiter. After he ordered, I said that in my law practice I never came in contact with the lucky and extreme cases he described and apart from that could only rarely catch a glimpse of them. 'If you could do it often, they wouldn't be lucky cases, would they? I was getting at something that you won't understand – I hardly understand it myself – that we love all the more, and perhaps only really love, what we have hated.' That sounded too extravagant to me. I could think of nothing to say, so we ate our cheese in silence.

I was looking for a re-entry point. So he drew privately, I said; would he also reveal what he did for a living? He taught dead languages, he said, but that had nothing to do with what we were talking about now. We fell silent again, until finally I said that before he'd gone up to his room he had used the expression 'too tame,' and in a comparatively loud voice, so that it still rang in my ears. Would he...? 'Right,' he interrupted me. 'We eat, drink, excrete, turn a blind eye and shrug our shoulders. Despite my advanced age and the shrug-like tremors that go with it, I'm forced to engage with world and time in a way that's harsher, more intense, more incisive, and to mistrust every tendency towards mildness. Who's to sniff out what's going on in the world, if the young stultify themselves with mere nervous busyness – apathy, in other words – and the old with mere forbearance? In short, I'm grimly determined not to become dull and tame, though I have to admit that my refusal to resign myself is not objectively, but only hygienically grounded, by which I refer to a hygiene of the soul, do you understand me?' 'Not very well,' I said, and Loos explained it as a simple matter. If his refusal to resign himself were objectively grounded, it would mean that he thought the lunacy that was part of the universal fabric was reversible and curable, that he believed in salvation, in other words, which was about as fatuous as the hope that the scent of jasmine would suddenly drift up from a sewer. Since he knew he couldn't change anything about the stink, at least he would call it by its rightful name and meet it, as it were, with open nostrils. He owed that to his soul. His soul, of course, felt mortified by its impotence, but – worse than that – would feel disgraced, if he shut the window and didn't give a damn about world and time.

Loos drank. I was amazed how much he could handle. He spoke with self-control, hardly ever raised the glass in toast, and sat like a rock. He did, however, sweat a lot and wiped his gleaming scalp with a handkerchief from time to time. 'You despise the world, don't you?' I asked. 'With all my heart,' he replied, without the least hesitation. 'I'm relieved, then,' I said, which ruffled his composure a bit. He scratched his neck and searched all his pockets for the lighter which lay in front of him on the table. 'You know,' I said, 'someone recently explained to me that hatred was the precondition of love.' Loos turned red, and just as I was beginning to worry that he would reach for the cheese knife again, he gave a short burst of laughter followed by a fit of giggling that he had to fight to control. His laughter lightened my mood and released the cramped tension his stony earnestness had made me feel. I felt I could risk treading a little more boldly. I asked him whether he might not be one of those failed idealists, so notorious in his generation, who resent the world for ignoring their dreams. Wasn't it perhaps easier to despise reality than to revise the wishful ideas he had of it as a youth?

Was he upset because I was annoyed when he condemned the world without having much more to bring against it than the fact that he was disturbed by the presence of mobile phones and hygiene bags or at least the advertising for what the bags held? Loos was silent. 'Where should I begin?' he finally asked and fell silent again. Then he said, 'This would be the place for some thunderclap of an utterance that would silence all objections with its originality and universal application. Isn't that what you expect? Unfortunately, I can't think of one. And I'm not going to revert to the bags and the exploitation of bodily fluids. We all know that everything gets marketed. In the midst of this furious marketplace, where by now practically every male and female presents him or herself as a market product that others have to outperform and displace – in the midst of this battlefield, I'm saying, the individual person feels, to the extent he feels at all, a little empty, a little overburdened, and very, very isolated. But now comes the godsend! The market doesn't leave its victims in the lurch. If you feel empty, it offers you entertainment, not, of course, gratis; if you're overburdened, you get an anti-stress programme plus ginseng capsules; and the isolated get mobile phones. Isn't that touching? Where do you get the idea that I hate the world because of mobile phones? Not that your insinuation is entirely false, Mr Clarin. It's true that some years ago, before the aforementioned boom in mobile phones began, I found them a nightmare, an intrusive example of the exhibitionism that was also just beginning to create a furore on the TV screen. I shared my aversion for them with many people I respected, and whom I still respect, despite the doodling that now emanates from their jacket pockets. But there's no longer any point in criticism, unless one wants to acquire the reputation of having an inflexible mind. But I'm boring you, aren't I?'

I said I asked him questions to hear answers. 'Thank you,' he said. 'I don't talk to people much since I lost my wife about a year ago. And when I do, I sense that people only listen to me out of politeness. So then. The moment some trend takes hold, no matter what lunatic features it has, it's already in the right. What many people do and approve of cannot be wrong: this is the logic, isn't it, the logic of idiocy, which itself declares every critic an idiot, doesn't it? – But I'm losing the point. What I originally wanted to say is that mobile phones repel me because they obliterate privacy and intimacy, and along the way raise the level of noise in the world. But I find it more repellent that you are not permitted to have reservations about them. If the virus – any virus – has infected everyone, then you can no longer call it a virus. In the beginning, yes, in the beginning you have any number of allies. But the more the current rises – and the more self-assured, hare-brained, and dictatorial it becomes – the more your allies topple over and fall into it. And while I stand dumbfounded on the bank, the last words they bellow out to me, in chorus, are: "Only those who change stay true!" Yes, people like me stand like fossilised geezers on the shore. So it is, Mr Clarin, and so it has ever been, which is why nostalgia is out of the question. I have learned early on, and from repeated experience, how friends who once wanted to jam the spokes of the wheel have become its suppliers of axle grease. Yet the dominant spirit of that time, which we in our spring days rightly felt to be dehumanising, still bore a stronger trace of humanity than the one these same friends later not only accommodated themselves to, but in various capacities helped push forward. To give one example, when the relatively controlled market began to throw off the fetters – went hog-wild, in fact, and showed with shameless honesty that it no longer needed morality even as a cover, and that it understood the concept of human dignity as a quaint relic of the dying left – many of my former comrades were already sitting in their executive chairs and joining right in, telling themselves that "only those who change stay true." And yet, Mr Clarin, there's recent cause for hope. I recently read in a business publication that a "lived humanity" was a good idea in the marketplace and in general. So, there's a new humanity in the offing, I thought. Then I read further and got a rash on my forearm. Humanity *pays*, it said, it has competitive advantages, it raises productivity. And you, Mr Clarin', – here Loos lost control and banged on the table with his fist – 'you insinuate that I hate the world because of hygiene bags and mobile phones!'

Loos immediately took hold of himself again and apologised for what he called his impulsive outburst. I asked him quietly if he really had the impression that our time was any more perverse than twenty-five to thirty years ago. He answered that he had already said the teary look backward was out of the question. Every period had its own novel mode of perversity, though there were of course epochs that strove to outdo others in infamy or imbecility. But as a basic principle he in no way regarded history as the history of a fall, that is, a process of ever-increasing misguidedness, nor was it a salvation history, where every-thing turns out for the best. Rather he saw historical development as a hectic exchange process: yesterday's evil is immediately replaced by today's new version. It was like foot and mouth disease: no sooner does it seem eradicated than mad cow disease breaks out. It's the way of the world, and the sum of evils remains approximately the same, that is, on a depressingly high level, only now they spread faster over larger areas, thanks to the global cannonades, so that within a few weeks practi-cally every child is playing on a Game Boy and almost overnight every woman is jumping into a pair of phosphorescent cycling tights or, as soon as the new decree goes out, three-quarter length leggings with a predatory-cat imprint. These were rather harmless and already dated examples, he said, but indicative all the same.

I asked Loos if his wife had worn bike tights or leggings. He said no. 'You see, that's what bothers me,' I said. 'You make these sweeping judgments. You regard cycling tights as an evil – fine, that's your right. But you make as if the evil were ubiquitous, as if there were nothing else besides. I'm convinced that if someone gave you nine roses, you would only see the one that was a little damaged, and if someone praised the eight intact ones, you'd think him blind or stupid. People who see things your way would necessarily conclude that the world is a har-rowing place, and one wonders how and why they would endure such bleakness.' 'If,' answered Loos, 'you compare the world to a bouquet of roses, then please at least preserve the right proportions. Of your nine roses it's really eight that are damaged, at best one is whole. So who has the more accurate perception, the one who sees the bouquet's dubious condition or the one who rapturously praises the single rose that's beyond censure?' 'Quite apart from the question of right proportions,' I said, 'one answer comes readily to mind: the person with the most accurate perception sees both. Flaws sharpen the eye for perfection, and perfection for flaws.' 'Not bad, not bad,' Loos said, 'only a little too easy. You forget the crucial point, which I will gladly demonstrate with your own example. Let's assume there are four roses objectively in the most perfect condition, and five are objectively damaged. If we allow ourselves to think that everyone would see it so, because it's so obvious, we will be wrong. All you have to do is hammer it into people's heads, as insistently as possible, that the damaged roses are splendid specimens, and the perception will correspond – people will experience the withered as fresh and full, and vice versa. Not all, of course, but generally so many that those who trust their own eyes and judgment begin to feel alien and even wonder whether they aren't doomsayers, complainers, and blowhards after all.' 'Excuse me, Mr Loos, but if in this present pluralistic age people come along claiming they know what good and bad and right and wrong are, then they really are blowhards. We need to ask them where they get the criteria that allow them to make their so-called objective judgments.' 'You indirectly confirm my point,' Loos answered. 'You're also one of the Zeitgeist surfers. First people get inoculated with the idea that everything is arbitrary and relative, and then they declare that others who insist on accountability are either blowhards or, even worse, bumpkins.' 'All right, fine,' I appeased him. 'But I'd just like to know what you base your value judgements on.'

Loos smoked, drank, and considered. Then he said, 'Let's take people instead of roses and take a look at other times and places. It has always been child's play to convince the members of group X that the members of group Y are nothing but rats and should be exterminated. You just have to say it loud and long enough, and you'll find as many men as you like who have just been waiting for the encouragement to deliver the deathblow, and just as many women who will foam at the mouth in screaming their approval. I regard this state of affairs as horrendous, and if you're curious about what I base that value judgement on then I'll have to leave this table.'

I didn't find his threat congenial, I said, and besides it was superfluous, since it would never cross my mind to ask anyone on what grounds he found inhumanity inhumane. I had asked him, Loos, where he got the criteria that allowed him to pass judgement on the trends, currents and fashions of the time, which were open to the most varying assessments according to point of view. The discussion had never been about atrocity, and as far as the rat principle was concerned, I was fully of his opinion, but I still had the impression, as I had said, that he looked only at the horrors that existed, and that is why I asked the question as to how and why he could stand it here. And included in this question was naturally another: whether the bright and the beautiful also existed for him? 'And whether,' said Loos, without having to consider, 'and whether, Mr Clarin, it's the same case with music – at least that's how I felt until recently, and actually still feel, in spite of the troublesome experience I had with it. Recently, you see, I spent a whole night listening to Mozart, the most buoyant, most magnificent things, and yet I couldn't get rid of my disgust with the world, couldn't overcome it. Just the opposite: the music made it clear to me that beauty is no consolation for but rather evidence of misery. It tries to make me forget the outside world and the rules that apply there, but precisely in so doing it recalls them. Or take Haydn's *Creation* – you don't have to be sentimental to be forced to tears when you hear certain passages, but you don't know whether you're weeping because of the beauty of the music, because of the resounding praise of the Creator, or because of the chasm that exists between praise of the Creator and the mutilated creation. The main thing is that you weep, isn't it, that you're shaken and softened, and you notice that you're not a stone, although...'

'Although?' Loos blew his nose and said, 'Although that too has disadvantages, since the human stone lives more independently of the weather. But however that may be, memory too belongs among the bright and beautiful things you're asking about, and I mean the memory of my wife, of our life together, of particular moments, words, gestures. It's beautiful to remember beautiful things, but even that doesn't come without pain, since you can't recall the beautiful without feeling the wounds its loss has opened up. Which brings me to your other question: how and why I can stand it here. You might have asked outright whether it isn't more sensible for someone like me to arrange his own removal. I think about it all the time and am certainly ramshackle enough for it. I lack neither the rage at life nor the inclination to withdraw from it all. And believe me, dissolving into nothing is not a prospect of terror for me. And yet I hesitate. Are you familiar with Kleist? I feel a kinship with him, and his sole theme was the fragility of the world's structures. But consistent as he was, he was inconsistent at the end, for just before laying hands on himself, he wrote in his suicide note: "The truth is that there was nothing on earth that could help me." That can only mean, "If I feel overtired, lay it not to the world, but to myself and my poor blood." But that's just it, suicide notes tend to be hopelessly polite – they take the blame on themselves and exonerate the world. Shouldn't the last *communiqué* sound much harsher? I would find it perfectly acceptable if Kleist had written: "The truth is that on this earth only criminals feel at home." But that would have been, first, self-praise, and second, an insult to those who were content to live, whom he wanted to think well of him, wouldn't it? But as for me, I hesitate, as I said; and by the time I get to the point where I could extinguish myself in the way I have in mind, that is, serenely and almost as casually as you would pull up a stalk of grass from the roadside – by that time nature will presumably have done the necessary on its own. And there's one more consideration. As enticing as the end might be, it would be just as irresponsible for me to leave my beloved wife alone, abandoning her to the horror unprotected.'

Loos blew his nose again, and I said, 'Now you've got to help me:

is your wife not dead after all?' He remained quiet, looking at me with eyes that struck me as feverish. 'Dead, yes,' he then said, 'but not properly buried, as it were. When I speak of abandoning her, it's in a rather obscure sense. What I was trying to say is, "Who will love her, if I no longer exist, who will still remember her, who will honour and preserve her memory in this age without memory?" You understand me now? Only if I live is she taken care of.' He wants to protect her beyond the grave, I thought and said, 'Yes, I understand, only I find it strange that you largely define your life as a service to someone you've lost. It seems to me that you take the mere acceptance of loss as an act of faithlessness. That must cripple you; it means stasis. You have a right to your own life and everything that goes with it.' Loos wasn't listening. He sat turned away, his gaze directed at the dark hills across the valley. 'Fresh raspberries,' he said aloud into the night and then fell silent again. Were there still earthly pleasures for him? I asked whether he would like some raspberries, should I order them if there were any? 'Over there, above, almost all the windows are lit now. We had our pre-execution meal in the dining hall at the health spa in Cademario, and my wife saw on the menu that they had raspberries as a dessert. We had started on the late side, and she was very worried that there wouldn't be any left by the time we were through with the main course. And although I realised that she saw this as a catastrophe and expected me to do something about it, I saw no solution. That's when she showed me how useless I was. She told the waiter she would like them served immediately, as an appetiser so to speak. She was very practical – she relished life so, things like eating raspberries.' 'And why "pre-execution meal"?' I asked. 'Because it was our last one. You can't imagine how I hate her sometimes for the way she simply disappeared after twelve years of marriage, years of love all in all – dissolved, stole away, and left me a survivor on this barbarous planet. And all the while she was well on the road to recovery: they had removed the tumour, there was no metastasis, and the blonde hair that had to be shaved off before the operation was quickly growing back under her scarf.' 'What happened?' I asked hesitantly. 'I can't speak about it right now.' After a pause, I said, as something that might interest him, that the girlfriend I had once sat with here had also been a patient at Cademario. 'I can't speak about it,' Loos repeated. 'I've said too much already. God knows why I abuse a stranger with my private concerns. Shall we order a last half litre?' 'You're not abusing me. The only thing is, how am I going to make the curves up to Agra if I drink any more?' 'On foot, that'll make you sober, and tomorrow you'll sit fresh at your desk and write – about what, though, has escaped me.'

That wasn't important, I said, and I said it not because his temporary absentmindedness had disgruntled me, but because I suddenly attached almost no further significance to my plan. Since Loos insisted on an answer, I explained again that it had to do with divorce law, or more precisely with the variations in the formulation of laws touching divorce in individual cantons from the Helvetik to the beginning of the 20th century. He probably knew that the uniform civil code for the whole confederation was still a relatively recent phenomenon, in force only since 1 January 1912, to be exact. Before that most of the cantons had had their own civil codes, and it was their relevant passages that were the subject of my work.' 'What a coincidence,' said Loos. 'That's also my father's birthday. But do you think you can do that over Pentecost?' 'I can't swear to it, but, first, writing comes easy to me, not least because of my two-year stint as a court clerk; second, I'm lucky enough to have an excellent memory; and third, I've got all the material with me.' 'You lugged half a library with you to Ticino?' Loos asked. 'What do you think? Just a single disk,' I said smiling. 'Ah yes, of course,' he said. 'Excuse me, I sometimes still think in old gross-sensory categories, which has recently been strengthened by my contentious relationship with Windows 2000.' I kept an uncertain silence, while Loos filled the glasses. He said he needed my expertise and advice. I asked what about. He said it was about how he could get rid of Windows 2000 so he could go back to working with Windows 98 again. It turned out that after installing Windows 2000 he could only run his trackball as a PS-2 mouse with two click-keys. Added to this was the sad fact that his Page Scan didn't want to scan anymore, nor his tape drive make backups. Also his Wizard Creator refused to function – in short the whole configuration that ran perfectly under Windows 98 was virtually down the drain. I stared at Loos. For a few moments I saw him in double, in fact a trick of the light had given him a moustache that looked like a black bird with outstretched wings over each of his two mouths. I eventually said that I had to pass, I had no idea. 'No problem,' said Loos, 'I know the answer.' 'You wanted to test me then, or make a fool of me,' I said. 'Not at all, Mr Clarin. I only wanted to shine a bit, to impress you, but above all to let you know that a person doesn't have to be a digital dummy or a yesterday yahoo to sometimes wish the whole electronic information-age shebang would go to the devil. You know what I sometimes imagine, lying on my sofa? The world after the lights go out all over the planet. All systems out, all batteries dead – the global clatter silenced. Still, ash-grey monitors. Stupefied people separated from the gadgets that had become part of their organisms, torn out of their shadow-world and blinded by the effulgence of other people! Are you even listening?'

In fact, while Loos seemed to be growing ever more wakeful, I had almost nodded off and was hearing his voice as if from a distance. 'No, I am,' I said, suppressing a yawn. 'You wanted me to think you're not stuck in the past, but then sketched a scenario that belies you.' 'That's right,' said Loos, 'that's the dilemma of today's sofa-dreamers: if you start from the existing situation, without tampering with it, if, that is, you stand on the platform of the status quo and imagine yourself in the future – hoping to envision a better reality – you're going to fail, because today's factual situation, which is necessarily implied by the dream, will then be three times more factual. There's no place to lodge your castles in the air any more. Dreams of the future, in other words, can only be nightmares, at least for those who are already horrified by the present. And if you dream these away by decreeing from your sofa a partial deluge to overtake mankind, then you'll naturally land back in yesterday's world. You'll have to swallow the reproach of backwardness. If you want everything to be slower, quieter, more sensuous, less shrill, you have no other choice than to imagine yourself back in the past. As I said, the future will be so powerfully real that cherished dreams no longer dare move forward, do you understand?'

'Yes, I understand,' I said, 'which doesn't mean that I have any sympathy for your attack on the electrical power system, which incidentally would hit you hard too: no more Haydn and Mozart at night.' 'Oh God,' Loos said, 'I hadn't thought of that, but I can get around it. In a pinch I'll make my own music.' 'Wine,' I continued, 'will be hard to come by, and cigarettes too, if only because of the collapsing logistics.' 'You're torturing me,' Loos said. 'You're ruining the deluge for me – that isn't nice.' 'I'm only warning you about the consequences for yourself.' 'Good,' he said, 'then we have to carefully consider where we can still wish ourselves. Forward, no storage space for dreams; backward, romanticism with scarcities; and in the middle, the tumid lunacy that makes us want to escape in the first place. What to do?' 'I know,' I said, 'we should leave now.'

When we finally stood up – to the relief of the staff, since we were the last to leave – I almost lost my balance. Loos, also swaying a little, but more self-possessed than I was, saw and offered to accompany me back to Agra. I said I appreciated the offer but he could go to bed without worrying. He said it was not a question of an offer, but of a need. 'I'm still fine to drive,' I said. 'It's practically all uphill. Downhill would be more ticklish.' 'Come on,' said Loos, 'no dramatics.' I got the flashlight out of the car's glove compartment, while Loos stood beside me and said, 'Ah, a Cabrio.' 'Used,' I said, and tossed the flashlight, which didn't work, back into the car. 'We even have a half-moon,' he said, hooking his arm under mine and pulling me along. After a few steps he abruptly let go, as if startled by the sudden closeness. We walked through the village without speaking, but before the small kiosk next to the post office he stopped and said that they sold postcards of Hesse's watercolours there; his wife had really liked them.

'And you?' I asked. 'What do you think of them?' For him, he said, whatever his wife had once liked was somehow sacrosanct. 'Was that the case while she was alive?' I asked, as we walked on. If it was impossible for him to share her liking, he said, he nevertheless gave the object credence and could sense what was worth liking about it. And if she had one day brought home a garden gnome? You usually know before marriage whether your chosen partner is likely to bring home a garden gnome, Loos said. And incidentally his wife liked Hesse's literary work as much as his watercolours, probably because she was something of a seeker, and Hesse is an excellent venue for seekers – you could open his books to any page and find some wise saying or rule of life, something that drove him, Loos, to desperation, whereas his wife had made a collection of such sayings in a small, squared notebook. But he didn't mean to sound mocking; as he said, he always respected his wife's predilections, and when she once, about two years ago, expressed the desire to drive down with him to Montagnola for a weekend to visit the Hesse Museum in the Torre Camuzzi, he had readily agreed. Nevertheless – as he had to acknowledge once inside this small and really very charming museum – the exhibited relics, such as Hesse's spectacles or the telegram from Adenauer on the poet's 75th birthday, had not especially moved him, least of all Hesse's umbrella. Yet it was precisely this that seemed to have positively captivated her.

Loos stopped walking and breathed heavily. 'Since being alone I've started smoking again, and that takes its revenge,' he said. 'I didn't smoke for five years, although my wife – she herself was a non-smoker – never pressured me to stop. It was an obese woman who freed me from my addiction.' 'A layer-on of hands?' 'No, not a layer-on of hands, but a person who sat across from me in a café and gobbled up various desserts with well-nigh shameless voracity. I felt disgust. 'How can someone be so unrestrained and weak-willed?' I asked myself, lit a cigarette, and realised that I was smoking it voraciously. That was my last, and in the next five years there was no backsliding. All right, we can march on as far as I'm concerned.'

'I'm still interested in this business of Hesse's umbrella,' I said. 'What about it impressed your wife so much?' He had asked himself that, Loos said, especially since it was just a simple black umbrella like his own and millions of others. In fact, he had not only asked himself, but his wife too, later in the hotel room – they were staying at the Bellevue. He, her husband, he told her, also had an umbrella, but evidently she regarded his as the epitome of commonplace, whereas she had stood before Hesse's umbrella as before a sacred object. Could she tell him what enchanted her about this umbrella? She smiled at him and reminded him of the Freud Museum they had visited together in Vienna; there was a display of one of Freud's half-smoked cigars that he, in contrast to her, had gazed on almost devoutly. He had to admit she was right – the cigar had indeed moved him intensely. And that was the end of that subject. In bed, his wife also read him a poem she was very fond of, that had been displayed in the museum, printed on a letter-sized sheet. Two lines of it she read to him three times, which is why he knew it by heart:

And so the heart at every call from life
Must ready be to part and start anew.

When she asked him if that wasn't beautiful, he had tactlessly grunted sleepily, at which she had turned the light out.

It pleasantly surprised me that Loos could not only harangue and debate, but all at once tell a story as well. And since he had so far divulged so little about his life, I now seized the moment and asked him whether school was fun for him, did he like teaching? He enjoyed being in the classroom, he said, but right outside the door an evil spirit ruled. Over the past few years schools almost everywhere had fallen prey to the bureaucrats, pedagogical illiterates; but on this march through the silent night any further word on the tragedy of the school system was forbidden.

We didn't speak again till we had the winding ascent behind us and had reached the plateau of the Collina d'Oro. The stars were gone, and a wind came up. 'What are you thinking?' asked Loos. 'Ah,' I said, 'I was just trying to remember when exactly I ended the relationship with the girlfriend I told you about.' 'Yes,' he said, 'it can't be easy for you to keep track. Is it so important?' 'Not at all. It just suddenly struck me that this girlfriend, who was also a patient at Cademario, might have known your wife, if they stayed there at the same time.' 'My wife was only there for five days, till the eleventh of June last year, if that helps you.' 'That means till the day after tomorrow a year ago?' 'Yes,' he said quietly, 'the accident's a year old on Pentecost.' I didn't dare ask again about the circumstances of her death and told myself that I would have heard from Valerie, who stayed at Cademario for three weeks, about any fatal accident that took place during her time there, all the more so if she knew Loos's wife.

Just before Bigogno the first raindrops fell, lightning lit up the sleeping village, the crickets fell silent, and after the thunder I advised Loos to turn back. It wasn't a good thing to break off something once begun, he said, and besides a good six seconds had passed between the lightning and the thunder. If you divided that by five you'd know how far off the storm was – more than a mile in our case. So he wasn't going to turn back, but on the other hand, he'd be happy if he could step off the road for a minute. I said I'd been feeling the same need for some time now. We stepped to the side of the road, keeping a distance of about two yards. I told him that in my practice I had recently had a man wanting a divorce, who had been trained by his wife only to pee sitting down in the bathroom, to avoid splatter, and now after four years of compliance, the client suddenly felt her spoon-feeding was grounds for divorce. Loos didn't take it up; he was humming to himself. For the first time I felt the urge to ask him his first name. 'What are you humming?' I asked. '"O How Lovely Is Thy World," a Schubert song,' he said, 'one of my wife's favourites.' 'That I practically assumed,' I said. 'You certainly see the world differently.' 'So it is – people complete themselves harmonically.' Was this harmony never troubled by discord? I asked, as I zipped up my fly. 'So seldom,' he replied, 'that I haven't forgotten a single instance, least of all the last, which had to do with pickle jars.' 'Pickle jars?' 'With empty pickle jars,' Loos said, who was also finished now. 'The case might interest you, I mean as a lawyer. One day we found an empty pickle jar in the parcel-bin – what we used to call the milk-bin – of our mailbox, and the next day another. At first I took them as a kind of joke greeting, but after a month, by which time I had disposed of a dozen of them, I got upset. At the same time I realised that I was practically disappointed when a few days went by without a new one appearing. After another two months, my wife was still giggling and calling it a non-problem, while I had to put up with these pickle jars invading my dreams. At night I sometimes stood in the unlit kitchen alone, looking out over the scene of the crime, but the perpetrator never showed himself. "Enough," I said after the sixtieth jar, "I'm going to the police, before I go crazy." "Do you know what you are?" my wife said, and her eyes for whole moments betrayed anger, if not contempt. "You're a wet blanket," she said. So of course I didn't report it, and my wife took over the duty of getting rid of the jars. And now I ask you, Mr Clarin, to give me a legal view of the matter.'

'Not easy,' I said. 'Did the perpetrator enter your property, or was your mail box on the side of the road?' 'The latter,' said Loos. 'Then by the criminal code trespassing hardly comes into consideration. On the other hand, you could appeal to the environmental protection law, which forbids waste-disposal except in approved repositories. For the inconveniences you suffered, you might have a claim to compensation according to the Code of Obligations, but, as I said, the case is hard to categorise. You did well not to take it to court.' 'Thank you,' said Loos. 'You're well-versed. Do you have a card? By the way, there was an end to the haunting, soon after my wife took charge. One evening, she put a jar *with* pickles in the parcel-bin, and it must have unsettled the delinquent so much that he never came back.' 'Did he take the pickles?' 'No,' said Loos, 'he probably thought they were poisoned.' 'You had a smart wife.' ' Yes, she was life-smart, in contrast to me, and superior to me in many ways, though she was twelve years younger. Most of all, though, she was placid; which is why, as I said, it very seldom came to heated words and only once to words like *wet blanket*.'

Loos was panting, so I slowed the pace. The storm didn't seem to have come any nearer, but no sooner had I concluded that we would reach Agra halfway dry than a violent downpour erupted. We were immediately soaked, so that it made no sense to seek shelter anywhere. We stopped talking. Only at the front door – Loos fired his lighter so I could find the keyhole – did I ask him whether he would like a night-cap. 'You're just asking to be polite. You have a lot to do tomorrow.' 'At the moment, I'm completely awake,' I said, truthfully. We went in. Loos looked around shyly. 'I can't offer you any dry clothes,' I said. 'You wouldn't fit in them. But please, sit down. I'll make a quick fire.' 'Excuse me,' he said, 'I think I'd rather go. I see that it's time.' 'That's a shame,' I said, and was genuinely disappointed. 'We could certainly meet again tomorrow, if you'd like, maybe in the evening,' he said. I replied, again truthfully, that it would delight me and that I had planned anyway to wait until evening to get the car. We drank a cognac standing. I thanked Loos for walking me home.

Outside, the crickets were chirping again, the rain had let up, and the breaking clouds gave us a quick view of the moon. 'Have a good trip back,' I said. 'Rest well,' he said, and his figure, a swaying bearlike shadow, lost itself in the dark.

Although it was already close to one, I made a fire in the fireplace. Then I took my wet clothes off and stood before it in my bathrobe. I wanted to think the whole experience over and clarify my scattered impressions of Loos. But instead, I fell into an unusual state of brooding over myself. I suddenly had the feeling that I lacked real feelings, that I was lukewarm, shallow. I was somebody I didn't like. From time to time a log crackled and threw off a few sparks. I drank another cognac.

At a certain point I was shivering, and pushed the embers back and went to bed. I slept badly, a rare occurrence.

II

NOT A RESTORATIVE SLEEP THEN, although I – otherwise an early riser – lay a full twelve hours in bed and only got up around two, with cricks in both mind and body. And yet I had planned to get to work at nine, so that to my headache and discontent was added the self-contempt that afflicts habitually disciplined people when they fail to do what they've resolved to do out of weakness of will. It was noticeably cool in the house, and while I lit the heater in the study, I recalled the suspicion that first occurred to me in my half-sleep, that Loos's wife might have killed herself. This seemed even more certain to me now that I was awake; it plausibly explained Loos's reluctance to talk about the circumstances of her death. I made myself a strong coffee. But do people who have been operated on successfully and released to recuperate in a sanatorium take their own lives? And hadn't Loos said that his wife relished life? I stepped out the door. It was cloudy. It didn't look like it was going to be a very pleasant Pentecost. The marriage must have been happy – a stroke of luck, according to Loos. Maybe a post-operative embolism? And there are also post-operative depressions, so possibly a suicide after all? I stood cleaning my spectacles – and felt anxious about dropping them. After another cup of coffee I went into the study and sat in front of the laptop, but after ten minutes I realised that I couldn't get into it, that there was a fog separating me from the screen and keyboard.

I went back into the kitchen area, sat down before the cold fireplace, saw a big spider running over the floorboards, and jumped up and smashed it dead with my slipper. Mental defect. Loos has a mental defect, I thought, without knowing where the expression had come from. I wrote it down on a block of note paper. I jotted down words, sentences, and scraps of sentences spoken by Loos or to him, in no specific order or connection. I felt cold and went into the adjoining shed to split some logs. Maybe I'm too normal, I thought. But that's far better than being half crazy, I also thought. His cult of the dead! It wouldn't surprise me if he kept her urn on his night table. Sometimes he repels me, other times I think I'm feeling something like what a son must feel towards a fragile father. I lodged the axe in the splitting-stump and went back to the study to give it another try. At any other time, I could have shaken a few introductory remarks on theme and purpose out of my sleeve even *with* a hangover. But now, though I was passably back in gear thanks to coffee and Alka-Seltzer, it was beyond me.

Of course I immediately thought of calling off the meeting with Loos, so that I could devote the evening to work and continue with it early on Pentecost Sunday with a buoyant mind. Why didn't I? Certainly not out of politeness or consideration. Loos didn't need me. He wasn't in my opinion like some sailor who needed an audience for his stories, and not even his condemnation of the world seemed dependent on finding an echo, much less approval, in someone else. It could even be that my company weighed on him and he now regretted yielding to the twinge of alcohol-conditioned affection that had led him to suggest a second meeting, and this on the eve of the anniversary of his wife's death, an evening which I imagined he would have wanted to devote to undisturbed remembrance. So everything spoke for calling it off – except, obviously, the one factor that proved decisive, although it wasn't really clear to me till the moment of the actual decision. Loos attracted me. More precisely and with fewer suspect connotations: I sought his aura despite myself. I call this phenomenon magnetism, even – as far as I'm concerned – magic. No more on that.

I went back to the kitchen and cleaned the oven, which my predecessor and co-owner had forgotten to do over Easter. I leafed through a women's magazine, which, I remembered, came from when Valerie was here. Recent investigations had now decided the question of whether women choose men according to looks. Their ideal of male attractiveness varies with their menstrual cycle, I read: in the fertile phase they prefer manly men with muscles and broad shoulders, during the rest of the cycle it's the more sympathetic type. The rest of the cycle is the main period in point of duration though, I thought, but did a few push-ups nonetheless. Another article cited a study according to which both men and women regard people with blue eyes as more attractive and intelligent than those with brown or green eyes – a finding that favoured me. When I put the magazine down my eye fell on its date of issue, June 21st of the previous year. Shortly after this date – in other words, two weeks after the death of Loos's wife – I must have picked Valerie up at Cademario, brought her here for an aperitif, and then driven her down to the Bellevue. Since this, as I knew for a fact, had taken place toward the end of the third and last week of her stay there, and since Loos's wife had died on June 11th after a five-day stay, I was able to conclude that the two women must have been at the Cademario Sanatorium together during their first week. Although it was clear to me that they could not have come to know each other – the sanatorium is after all enormous, and otherwise Valerie would, as I said, have told me about the death – my discovery brought me to a state of excitement that I could hardly explain. Irrationally, I seemed to feel that as Loos's wife and Valerie might for a few minutes have seen and smiled at each other, this bound me closer to Loos. He himself had of course made it known, tersely, almost gruffly, that such coincidences didn't interest him, which made me resolve not to bother him with it. And it was still unclear whether I would have another conversation with him. 'We could certainly meet again tomorrow,' Loos had said verbatim. I remembered that as exactly as I did much else that he had said. The old saying about wine – that it kills memory – was never, or hardly ever, true of me. This 'meeting' could mean a handshake, a short goodbye, but also another meal together. What was my preference? I wasn't really sure, but then definitely inclined to the latter. Perhaps it's like a reader who would like to put down a book that's short on plot, but eventually keeps reading it, either because he hopes or suspects that the decisive event is still coming or because the half-experienced, the broken-off and unfinished, gives him an unsettled feeling. The comparison limps, of course, in the sense that I myself could not, or would not, decide whether the conversation was to continue – Loos's situation and his seniority unquestionably gave him the right of option. And as far as unsettled feelings go, I have them all the more now that I've read the book. I wish they were merely unsettled.

The rest of the afternoon I spent in utter idleness. I sat or walked around the house, picked up a piece of lint, blew a crumb from the table, which I stooped to pick up again after another walk through the house. I hate inactivity, it puts me under stress. 'Lord, let it be evening!' An exclamatory prayer no one had ever yet heard issuing from my mouth. And now I heard it myself, and it was answered in the usual way, so that I was able to start out at close to six equipped with an umbrella and haunted by a vague sense of foreboding.

The terrace was empty, with just a waiter busy drying off the wet tables and chairs. When he saw that I was looking at him, he glanced several times up at the overhanging sky with a sceptical expression that seemed to say he was aware of the apparent futility of what he was doing. I asked if I could get an aperitif. He nodded, and I settled myself at the same table as on the previous evening, but in the seat Loos had sat in, and when the waiter went to bring the Campari I looked up at the façade of the hotel – and froze. The window of the room Loos had pointed out as his stood open, and though it wasn't a rifle but a telescope I saw pointed at me, I felt very uncomfortable, even threatened. But before I could get really angry at Loos, he appeared in the window and waved to me – apologetically, as I took it – and shortly afterwards he stood before me, embarrassed. 'That was tactless,' he said. 'Please excuse me. I was trying to penetrate the mist, when I saw you and couldn't resist bringing you in my sights for a minute. I'm sorry. My telescope otherwise serves only to bring the

Cademario Sanatorium close. You're downright pale. How are you feeling?' 'Frankly, mediocre,' I said. 'And you?' 'I'm in a playful mood, God knows why,' he said and sat down across from me. In truth he did look different than on the previous evening, more relaxed and cheerful. He beamed accessibility. 'You *are* staying for dinner?' he asked. 'Gladly,' I said, 'as long as you wouldn't rather be alone.' 'I wouldn't have asked in that case. I rarely allow myself to be governed by feelings of duty any more. The older I get, the more fastidiously I select them and follow only the few that halfway agree with my inclinations. By the way, I've reserved a table inside, since there's little prospect of a dry evening. Why are you feeling mediocre?' I told him about my trying night, about my lingering in bed and my chagrin over it, and about my sluggish, wasted day. There were no wasted days, Loos said, and lack of drive, understood as civil disobedience, as a counterforce to the great hustle and bustle, was a symptom of health. Everything that served to slow us down, even a prolonged breakfast, benefited the public health, which was endangered as never before, because more and more people felt that they were no longer equal to the frantic pace of mechanisation and were falling by the wayside. Whether or not they wanted to admit it, whether or not they smoothed it over with last-ditch agility and cheerful panache, they were all utterly and unremittingly overburdened, and that made for sickness. Take the animals, by contrast. No animal on earth worked, with the exception perhaps of ants, bees and moles, whose busyness, however, was not motivated by a moral imperative. The others sauntered around here and there in their search for food – unless we took house pets like cats and dogs. The average dog, for example, slept or dozed for about twenty hours a day, and cats took it just as easy. He and his wife, in fact, had had a cat, a black one with white paws. His wife had loved it, but he sometimes had a hard time countenancing its unspeakable laziness. All it did was let itself be served and then sink back, purring, into a half-sleep, while he had to watch the clock and leave for work. But at least these animals, in contrast to human beings, were healthy and had a sleek coat of fur.

'Mr Loos,' I said, 'it was a perfectly normal hangover that put me out of action, and you do it all too much honour to interpret it as an expression of civil disobedience and make it a pretext for an excursus on animals and public health.' Loos ordered a glass of white wine, saying nothing until it arrived at the table. He was aware of his propensity to excursus, he said; his wife had often alluded to it. He also dimly remembered having already spoken about overburdenment yesterday. So he was repeating himself. Excursus and repetitions were an imposition on any interlocutor, and since he couldn't promise to refrain from either, politeness behoved him to retire now.

Loos was serious. He stood up and gave me his hand. I kept hold of it, disconcerted, and finally told him I had been very much looking forward to my evening with him. 'Really?' he asked. 'Really,' I said, and lied a bit when I added, 'What you feel as an imposition doesn't disturb me in the least.' Loos sat down and emptied his glass. He took up the thread again calmly, as if nothing had happened. He hardly knew anyone who was not marked by fear of failure. Almost all of us, to use a crude image, had a load in our pants, and just as real incontinence falls prey to shame and silence, so our anxieties about failing remained well cloaked. Whatever context we moved in, we were dealing with nothing but poor souls who in secret required most of their energy to keep their stigma veiled. There was little prospect of a mass coming-out; nor, consequently, of a revolution of the overburdened. In contrast, what was in prospect – was indeed already a fact – was a proliferation of psychological malaise of unprecedented epidemic proportions. And despite the massive use of chemical aids and the colourful palette of other cures and promises of cures, the root of the problem remained untreated, the wretchedness raged on.

'Do you tolerate objections?' I asked Loos. 'I may be a know-it-all,' he answered, 'but I do crave dissent.' 'Good,' I said. 'I told you that my plan was to devote myself to my divorce-law project today, but that then, instead of getting up early, I stayed in bed, and in the early afternoon, wreck that I was, I couldn't get anything else going. This lack of drive – or, more accurately, weakness of will – filled me with discontent, even with self-contempt. So, this was the pretext for your disquisition, the gnat you turned into an elephant. Your overburdened-society thesis may well be correct, and is hardly brand new, but it has nothing to do with my case. That's one thing, and as to the thesis itself: yesterday you stated that you were not a historical pessimist. In fact, so you said, the sum of evils remains approximately constant, since every old one is replaced by one of a different kind. I agree with that, and I also concede that feeling overburdened can be a source of unhappiness, but it's in no way a new source. There have always been over-burdened people – each age produces its own poor souls, and every society its own brand of psychological misery...' 'And because that has always been so,' Loos interrupted, 'a person should keep his trap shut, especially if he can't contribute anything "brand new" to the solution of the problem.' 'Absolutely not,' I said. 'May I finish?' 'I'm sorry,' he said. 'I'd like to remind you of a time,' I continued, 'that I, unlike you, know only from hearsay – I mean the evidently stuffy period of the 50s and early 60s. How tight-meshed the net of morality was then, how rigid the system of values, how reproachful the eye of God! Social control and repression on all sides, and an educational system that would slap your face to prove it only wanted the best, namely the expulsion of all feeling of self-worth, which was perceived as bare-faced impertinence, and the training of people to become not exactly failures – they don't achieve anything anyway – but rather creatures who *fear* failure and so do everything demanded of them. I ask you as a witness of that time: Is my appraisal correct?' 'It could have come from me,' Loos answered. 'It was the classic overburdenment society,' I said. 'Then came the fresh wind. The apron strings were cut: hair grew longer, skirts got shorter, and breath, walk and speech became freer. The relativising of morals unburdened the individual, and looser and broader ideas of value made new lifestyles possible – in short, the deregulation process of our worldviews has given us room for free play that is unprecedented in history. And yet it's your view that today's humanity is more overburdened and psychologically oppressed than ever, simply because the tempo of change is more than we can manage.'

'I could now say,' Loos ventured after a long pause, during which he ground his teeth, 'that it's the privilege of advancing years to see the new age with its new evils as far more misguided than the old. I could further say that it's up to each individual to evaluate evils as he chooses, since their magnitude can't be measured with a yardstick. But I won't say either, though it would show us in agreement. We are one only in our judgement of a musty period whose demise we welcome. But you are much more sanguine than I am about what followed. You don't enquire into the costs. You say nothing about the difficult situation of people who are freed from the leash and then, after a few leaps in the air, fall to brooding on where they should turn now in a landscape that is broad and colourful but without signs to mark the way. Put yourself in the place of a woman standing in front of her wardrobe in the year 1950. Two or three things hang there for weekdays, as well as a Sunday dress. She hardly hesitates, her reach is sure. The woman of today stands for a half-hour in front of an overfull wardrobe, a light vertigo takes hold of her, everything she reaches for seems wrong, and she usually concludes she has nothing to wear. Good! We can smile at distress of this kind. But now, does the woman have children to educate? According to what standards? By what methods? With what objectives? The range of offerings is broad and contradictory, and of limited significance. Do you know any parents who are not deeply insecure? Do you know any mother who does not feel she is doing almost everything wrong or, in retrospect, has done everything wrong. If we are cynical, we can say that these mothers, these parents, are right to feel they are failures, for look at their offspring – all with behavioural disorders, all unstable, capricious, disoriented zappers and surfers of their own lives. But as I said, that would be cynical, almost as if we were to blame the captain of a ship that had lost its navigation system through an act of God for not bringing his passengers back to dry land. In short, in the previous epoch we were moulded by a mandatory system of canonical values and a strict, narrow-minded morality; we were often contorted by it, and always overburdened. In our present day, the hierarchy of values has been suspended – they have been privatised to the point that it is up to each individual to choose which ones to follow. But perplexity grows as a result: there is nothing harder and more overburdening than to have to seek and choose without guidance. I won't go into further detail regarding the old and new modes of overburdening. I will only say, so that you don't place me in the wrong corner, that I think there is nothing sadder and more dangerous than the clamouring of emancipated slaves for orientation and a foothold – and possibly for the whip.'

Drops of rain were falling, but Loos seemed not to notice. He did pause, but I saw that he still had more to say. 'Well,' I said. 'Well,' he said, 'if we now add to the new form of overburdening that we've already mentioned the even newer form, which consists first in our vain and panting efforts to slow the stormy tempo of development in science and technology and second in our ashen-faced realisation that all the knowledge and understanding we have acquired today will be yesterday's snow tomorrow – then, I think, my claim of a psychological malaise of unprecedented proportions is not too outlandish. How will it proceed? Dare we hope for a revolution of the snails? What do you think?' 'I think it's raining,' I said, 'and that we should move.' 'It is indeed raining,' he said.

After we had taken our seats at the reserved table in the glassed-in annexe and received the half of white wine we had ordered, we toasted. 'To the revolution of the snails!' I said. 'To the early cracking of the rafters!' he said, gracing me with his ever so rare half-mischievous, half-melancholy smile. Since he craved dissent, I then said, I wanted to confront him with two empirical findings that must cast doubt on his diagnosis. The one was statistically substantiated, the other the fruit of my own observation. So then: a new representative survey – focused on the psychological, physical and material condition of the older generation – showed that this group, according to its own estimate, felt significantly better off than the same age group surveyed ten and twenty years previously. And on the other hand, the young, from approximately ages fifteen to thirty, exhibited a cheerful, pleasure-loving, fun- and satisfaction-oriented behaviour – nothing like the depressed, morose behaviour we would expect if his description of the situation were accurate. You only have to be present at a street parade to see how keyed-up and high-spirited so many young people are. And with regard to my own case, as a man in his mid-thirties, I was equally unable to help him with any malaise. I took life easy, and its shortness was a call for me not to despise its deliciousness.

Especially delicious, said Loos, pointing at the menu, was the filet of rabbit – he recommended it highly. 'Is that a displacement manoeuver or do you not take me seriously?' I asked. 'I did tell you I was in a playful mood,' he responded, 'and besides, I think we should order before I wind up for the counterpunch.' 'I'm familiar with it,' I said. 'With what?' he asked. 'The filet of rabbit. It was our parting meal out on the terrace.' 'I don't completely understand you,' Loos said. 'You probably didn't hear me when I told you that I was once here with a girlfriend who was a guest in the sanatorium across the way. I wanted to use it as a pleasant setting for suggesting to her that we break up. We both had a *filetto di coniglio* then.' 'Excellent,' said Loos, 'and why was she there?' 'Problems with her nerves, autonomic instability,' I said. Loos was quiet for a while. 'That brings us back to our theme,' he then said. 'The malaise has many faces, and a malfunctioning nervous system is one of them, a quiet and sympathetic one, though hard to bear for the one afflicted. More widespread, however, is another, which is really a mask, a form of expression that makes the suffering unrecognisable, namely, hectic cheerfulness. Your cheery youths, Mr Clarin, know instinctively what reflection and quiet would mean: a plunge into the maws of reality. Believe it or not, I was once on the sidelines watching a street parade, and what I saw was a funeral procession – true, a clangorous one.' 'So lust for life is a symptom of grief,' I said. 'Are you in your right mind?' 'In my right mind I am not, but that's no evidence for the nonsense of my interpretation. Even if I were a fool, you'd still have to grant me a sympathetic sense for what's foolish, for masquerades and disguises of every kind, for the mummery of the grieving psyche. It seems to me that your empirical eye doesn't distinguish between costume and disguise – hence your vehement protest. I'd like, in a fatherly sort of way, to give you a proverb that I picked up somewhere, to take with you on your path through life. I can quote its gist: "When you see a giant, ask yourself first if it's not the shadow of a dwarf."' 'Very nice,' I said, 'I'll take it to heart. But you should hold to it and not draw the false conclusion that *every* reality is mere illusion – in this case that all lust for life is disguised mourning. The existence of actual giants doesn't invalidate the proverb you quote.' 'Agreed,' said Loos. 'Let's go ahead and order now, that is, we can still quickly dispense with the happy seniors – I had almost forgotten about them. Which age group did the statistical findings describe?' 'Retirees of both sexes.' 'All right, so, retirees – granted, that's a sizeable group. I'm delighted that they feel better off than in earlier times, but it doesn't surprise me. They have the roughest time behind them, they're free from many constraints and better cushioned than before. Of the dumbing down of considerable numbers of the aged I say nothing, though it likewise contributes to their sense of wellbeing. However that may be, the results of the survey confirm my diagnosis, I mean because the degree of their wellbeing has to be measured against the dissatisfaction that preceded it. If retirees feel much better off than ever before, then the situation they have escaped must have been an unprecedented torment, no? And now we can give our order – I'll have the filet of rabbit.'

I followed suit. And because it seemed senseless to me to make another suggestion on that subject, the conversation faltered. He channels all streams to his mill, I thought, and collects evidence for the misery of the world with the obsession of any collector. 'It might seem,' he said now, 'that I'm bent on the shabby satisfaction of proving myself right, but it has to do with the fact that no one hears my second, beseeching voice, when I speak. And what it says, after each of my statements, is: "Dear world, please give me the lie."' 'And?' I asked. 'Does she give you an answer now and then?' 'Yes, but an evasive one that rather contributes to our sense of impotence. "You dear statements," she says, "you cannot grasp me. It's been quite a while," she says, "since I've allowed myself to be comprehended or portrayed. Sorry."' 'She could be right,' I said, 'and if she is, we'll just have to stop talking about her.' 'Just not so blusteringly, just not so meekly,' Loos responded. 'But we still have other possibilities, at least two: We can scold her and we can describe the impotence her heedlessly complex character makes us feel. And third, it has just occurred to me, there are statements that do not have the ambition of fathoming the world's constitution. Fortunately we can also talk about football, about dogs and causes of death, we can tell stories about what we've experienced, or heard, or invented. In short, we are, figuratively expressed, not dependent for a subject of conversation on the woman who has given us the cold shoulder. We have sufficient other material.'

Once the food was brought out, Loos closed his eyes for a moment, as he had done the previous evening, and only then picked up his knife and fork. After a few bites he paused and said that he was often sorry, when he had had a delicious meat dish, that his wife could never enjoy it with him, since she had given up eating the meat of warm-blooded animals. At the beginning, when they had been getting to know each other, shortly after her conversion to vegetarianism, she was overzealous like all converts and had even said, to his consternation, that she would not, on principle, kiss men who were meat-eaters. Thank God that love had subsequently proved stronger than her ascetical resolution, so much stronger that she, his wife, though she stayed with her vegetarian diet, occasionally prepared him chicken, lamb, a cutlet, etc, though always with the affecting anxiety that what she had cooked hadn't come out right. Of course that was never the case, just the opposite. Sometimes now, when he was about to eat, he saw her blue-green eyes fixed on him, filled with an anxious expectation. It was always her eyes that he saw first whenever he brought her to mind.

Luckily, I said, his wife had at least not given up drinking wine, and so could enjoy with him, for instance, the merlot bianco we were drinking. Loos stopped chewing, stared at me, swallowed, and asked how I knew that. Because yesterday, I said, when I had asked him whether he could recommend the wine he was drinking, he had given me the remarkable answer: 'We always found it congenial.' A person doesn't forget an answer like that, and so I had now simply concluded that his *we* meant himself and his wife. That was indeed true, said Loos. He had occasionally drunk a glass of wine with his wife here a year ago. I asked whether I could also conclude that he had accompanied his wife on her convalescent vacation. This was also a valid conclusion, he said, but he would be glad not to have to talk about it for the time being. How had my day been? 'I can only repeat,' I said, 'that my day was short and barren, I lacked oomph and a clear head, my work lay hardly touched, and my idleness spoiled my mood. My day was an un-day. And yours?'

'Mine began unpleasantly, otherwise I can't complain.' 'Hangover? Headache?' 'Not a trace,' said Loos, 'but after the alarm rang – which isn't a ring at all, of course, but a series of beeps, as with everything these days – I nodded off again for a few minutes and was plagued by a short dream, an SQS dream.' Loos chewed, and I asked if that was a special psychological term. It wasn't yet, he said, but would probably be one soon. SQS stood for 'Salary-effective Qualification System' and had even penetrated the classrooms under this bombastic title at the behest of the economic system and its cringing enforcers. This meant that for the purpose of judging a teacher's qualifications a 'visitor' dropped in from time to time, sat at a desk in the back, spread out various sheets and a checklist before him, and during the instruction evaluated the 'field competence,' the 'method competence,' and the 'social competence' of the teacher. To make a competent judgement of these three competences he had no less than thirty-nine criteria at his disposal. That he might know what actually belonged under the rubric of social competence, for example, there were eleven relevant points itemised on the checklist, among them the 'gestures' and 'facial expressions' of the teacher being evaluated, as well as – whatever it might mean – his or her 'role model effect.' Two further points were 'stamina' and 'humour,' both instances of salary-effective social competence that victims of this procedure often vainly struggled to achieve, to be sure! In short, Loos went on, before reaching for knife and fork again, if the Salary-effective Qualification System was already nightmarish enough as a neologism, how much more was it so for what it meant, and then, still more emphatically, for his dream of it this morning. 'What did you dream then?' 'Just the usual. I was late to class without being prepared, neither of which has ever actually happened. The pupils wouldn't talk, but chewed gum and sent and received text messages. The visitor made checkmarks and then took me aside after class to say in my ear that my nasolabial folds were too pronounced, which would mean a pay deduction – at which point I awoke. Unfortunately the nasolabial folds, popularly known as worry folds, obsessed me the whole day. On the walk I took in Lugano I felt compelled to scour every face I saw for them. But otherwise, as I said, my day was thoroughly tolerable.'

Yesterday on our night walk to Agra, I said, he had not been able to speak on the subject of school and had only alluded to tragedy. Was the qualification system he just described what he meant by that? Marginally that too, Loos said, for it was part of the barbarity that raged in the school buildings. Ever since the so-called education politicians had agreed that the school system had to become 'frontline-oriented' – an expression which incidentally said it all about the mentality of such people – the school buildings were echoing with the panting and wheezing of both pupils and teachers. But as long as a morsel of rabbit filet and a few beans still remained on his plate, any further word on the subject was off limits. The SQS had already curbed his appetite. There should on principle be no unedifying subject of conversation during a meal – his wife had taught him this, and they had stuck to it as a rule, though it had condemned him to a certain monosyllabicity, especially, of course, when he read the newspaper before eating. He would mention in passing that he was an addicted reader of the paper, but while the satisfaction of an addiction normally brought pleasure, in him it predominantly aroused disgust. Was that not a paradox? 'Only on first glance,' I said, 'since there are people who like to be disgusted and take a keen interest in the unpleasant.' 'You mean me,' said Loos. 'I have already had to defend myself several times against your suspicion, but nevertheless, on a very general level you are right: Without a minimal delight in filth no halfway sensitive person could read the newspaper without washing his hands afterwards. But we're still eating, excuse me, and my day was really wanting in dissatisfactions, as long as we discount the aforementioned dream and perhaps also my unsuccessful quest in the various shops of Lugano to find something that seems hardly to be produced anymore, because the textile industry shows ever less concern for the needs and habits of older people. For a full fifty years I have worn briefs with an opening or fly – it's *opening* in Switzerland, *fly* in Germany – but these briefs with an opening or fly have increasingly disappeared from the market. I've just remembered, my wife had a similar problem. For a while underwired bras were so in fashion that she had the greatest difficulty digging up a normal bra anywhere. She simply couldn't wear an underwired bra, because it would have reminded her of the most frightening incident in her life. But that that doesn't belong to our present conversation. I only wanted to say that normal briefs are being systematically squeezed out by underpants that are not fit for purpose, that have no fly and can thus hardly be distinguished from women's panties, so that we have to speak of a creeping feminisation in the area of men's underwear and the abolition of the distinction.' 'I beg you, Mr Loos, there are still boxer shorts, and they are free of any feminine touch!' 'I've tried them,' said Loos. 'They're too roomy for me, I get no feeling of security in them. But there it is exactly: the world is out of joint, and there is much we seek in vain therein.'

Loos paused. He looked embittered. Not the slightest facial expression betrayed that he saw anything ridiculous about his lament. Either he was a master of dissimulation or I was in fact dealing with an unbalanced person. But in spite of my alienation I lifted my glass and said consolingly, 'To the fly!' Now he smiled, reached for his own glass, and clinked with me. He then drank it down in a single draught. 'Basically, I'm in a jovial mood,' he said, 'because I also had a lovely, almost wondrous experience in Lugano. Shall I tell you about it, or would you welcome it if I were a little more reticent?' I asked in return whether he could really fail to imagine how curious I was to hear something that wasn't negative coming from his mouth for once. '"Accusation is my office and my mission,"' said Loos. Pathetic crackpot, I thought, and Loos said: 'Schiller, from *Wallenstein*.' And then he began to tell his story – the waiter meanwhile removed the plates. He had bought a newspaper from the kiosk at the railway station in Lugano. The woman had waited on him in a friendly way, just as the sign behind the glass with the words 'Guaranteed Friendliness' printed on it had indeed promised. He then passed two automatic booths for passport photos in the station's forecourt and immediately felt the urge to see himself in a photograph again. One of the booths was occupied, with the curtain drawn, so he sat himself in the other. He put his coins in the slot and with eyes opened wide braced himself for the flash, which startled him anyway. The person in the next booth came out at practically the same moment he did, an attractive woman of about forty, and she not only nodded to him, as he did to her, but smiled at him, and smiled to such a degree that he got embarrassed and started to sweat. While they were waiting for the photographs to develop they made eye contact several times – her gaze was warm and probing, his was probably rather shy, and he was always the first to look away. Nothing was said; he couldn't think of anything, since he had never been a man of the world. With respect to spontaneity he was a dilettante, as his wife had once told him, verbatim, but with indulgence. When the strip of four photos slid into the delivery chute he felt relieved and immediately pulled it out. It was still warm and a little moist. He looked at the pictures dumbfounded and simply couldn't believe that this image of a half-moronic criminal from a wanted poster was his own like-ness. True, he saw his face, when he looked in the mirror, as a shadowy autumnal landscape, but that didn't mean that he found it unbearable. Yet this face in the photo was an impertinence, and his dismay was at its peak when the woman, who had apparently been observing him and had meanwhile received her own photos, spoke to him.

Loos stubbed out his cigarette and used his handkerchief to wipe the sweat from his forehead and neck with elaborate care. He drank. He drank continuously, as he had the evening before. He didn't look like a criminal, so I find it really mysterious that when he pronounced the word, I was struck by the awful thought that he might have killed his wife. But no sooner did the thought occur to me than I realised its absurdity, and the only way I could justify the momentary suspicion to myself was to take it as a sign that my table companion was still a com-plete stranger to me and made me feel uneasy. To be sure, I'm inclined to expect anything of anybody on principle – no one with court expe-rience can do otherwise. And yet I was now embarrassed by my fleet-ing suspicion with respect to Loos, who in the first place did not look like someone on parole and, in the second, had spoken so affection-ately about his wife, about his harmonious marriage with her, that one could almost have felt envious. 'What are you thinking about?' Loos asked. 'Oh,' I said, 'not really about anything. I was only asking myself why people in these automat photos often look a little demented and even almost criminal and why this is more the case with men than with women.' 'Could it be,' Loos asked without looking at me, 'that you were thinking about something else?' I gulped and said no. '"Thoughts are free,"' he said, 'and by the way, your observation is on the mark: the woman I mentioned, in any case, looked in her pictures exactly the way she did *in natura*, that is, very fetching, not to say enchanting. But in sequence: I was about to go and was looking for a trash container, when the woman spoke to me, asking if she could see my pictures. I don't know what confused me more, her curious request or the similarity of her voice to my wife's. I stammered that the photographs were terrible, that they had come out so badly that it would embarrass me to show them to her. She smiled. She was wearing a loosely tied orange scarf on her head, a warm Indian orange, which likewise reminded me of my wife and of the awful time when they shaved her head. The woman said that she found failures intriguing. She didn't take up my "Why?" but took a step toward me and reached very, very gingerly for the photo strip in my unresisting fingers. "Let's sit down," she said and pointed at the metal bench next to the photo booths. There she looked at the pictures and said not a word. After a while she asked, "Can I have one of these?" "But why?" I asked. She said, "Must everything have a reason?" "Maybe not," I said, "only I'm not happy about giving myself away in such a disfigured form, or do you collect antic faces?" She rummaged in her handbag and took out a tiny pair of scissors. I was so flabbergasted that I didn't intervene: when she cut off one of the pictures, neatly and with a childlike absorption, I simply allowed it to happen. "And now the return gift," she said and cut off one of her own photos. She took my free hand, which was closed into a fist, folded each finger back, one after the other, and put the photo in my hand.'

Loos appeared agitated. He said he had to go up to his room for a minute. Only after he left the table did I notice that the light armless sweater he was wearing had been put on wrongly: the V-neck was on the back, and to the right of it, at shoulder height, was pinned a black mourning button. The sight might have amused me, but I found it somehow disturbing. Loos was gone a good ten minutes, and when he returned he looked different. He had had the urge to shave, he said; now he felt better. He had the sweater on properly now, and without the mourning button.

'I called my experience wondrous, which it also was,' he said, 'but it not only lifted me up, it bent me down at the same time.' 'Excuse me,' I interrupted, 'you haven't told the rest of the story yet. What happened next?' 'There was no next. I must have fled. I found myself back in the mail van to Montagnola, where I awoke from my daze without being able to recall how I had got to the stop. If we didn't know better, we might think the woman had bewitched me, don't you think?' 'My God, Mr Loos, what do you mean by "bewitched"? She was Circe herself, are you blind? She was practically forcing herself on you, or at least offering herself. And you, instead of gratefully snatching at the offer, take to your heels. It's really beyond comprehension!' 'Yes, it's hard to comprehend, Mr Clarin, especially for spontaneous natures and other ever-ready types, and on the other hand it's easy to understand and actually easy to explain. I belong, you see, to the lowest caste – since fate has taken my wife away – the caste of the untouchables. It still isn't completely clear to me at this moment who I'm confiding in. I hardly know you, you're young, and you're very different, and your aplomb with women doesn't exactly make it easy for you to understand me. But no matter, no matter. I say it loud: I'm handicapped!'

Loos really did say it loud, and the neighbouring table went quiet. I saw that Loos's hands – which by the way had nothing fleshy or pawlike about them, but in their delicacy contrasted strangely with his heavy physique – were trembling a little. I waited till the two couples at the next table resumed their conversation and then told Loos that the word *handicapped* sounded too strong; it was certainly rather a matter of a temporary cramping. He seemed to have so mercilessly excluded the erotic after the loss of his wife that now, when it brushed against him in spite of himself, he felt threatened and cramped up. That was understandable, but a shame, and would only become a handicap if he kept the barrier in place out of a mistaken sense of fidelity. Did he really think he was acting in the interest of his dead wife if he emasculated himself, so to speak, if he lived the life of a monk, perhaps to the end of his days?

There were things in the psyche, said Loos, that did not allow themselves to be governed, as was well known. There were inner handicaps that were independent of the will and therefore inaccessible to appeal, and for this reason my advice to let down the barrier, however well meant, was meaningless. Something in him was receptive to the erotic – he was a sensual man – and something in him performed acts of sabotage, whenever he neared the flame. I had erroneously interpreted this second something as a falsely conceived fidelity, but it was not a question of fidelity here, not even as rightly conceived. For fidelity sprang from an act of will, which is why it was felt to be a moral virtue. He, however, did not at all *will* the barrier, and he had incidentally only become aware of it because he had been ready in the last half-year, although seldom, to enter the terrain beyond.

'I have a friend,' I said, 'who is happily married, and he insists that he lacks for nothing, even in bed. And yet he nevertheless repeatedly gets involved with other women. He explains that his desire can't be focused on a single woman. In short, he takes certain liberties with fidelity, and has a very relaxed attitude to his extramarital affairs. So it seems in any case, so he has always represented it. But a short while ago, he came to me late in the evening, tipsy and forlorn. He told me he had been brooding on a certain question and could come to no conclusion. He asked for my opinion, as well as my discretion. His question was as follows: What does it mean when despite all erotic desire your member refuses to get hard except within the principal relationship?'

'I don't know what you're trying to say,' Loos said gruffly. 'My impediment isn't of a bodily nature. Why should I be concerned with the afflictions of a philanderer?' 'Well,' I said, 'they might show you that fidelity, counter to your idea of it, is not due to an act of will, but – how shall I say? – tied to a subconscious apron string. As much as your barrier might differ from my friend's, I interpret both as the consequence of an inner edict that insists on fidelity.' 'Isn't that a little trivial?' Loos asked. 'That may be,' I answered, 'but does the trivial have to be false?'

At that moment a mobile phone peeped. Loos shook his head and turned red. I feared an angry outburst. He reached for his jacket, which hung over the back of the chair. Now he's going to leave, I thought. He slid his hand into one of the outer pockets and the peeping stopped. 'Sorry,' he said, 'I forgot to turn it off.' 'No problem,' I said. 'You see,' he said, 'a person can honestly curse what he himself takes part in – life for example. Your health!' 'A cheer for inconsistency!' I responded, 'It keeps us flexible.' 'It robs us of our self-esteem, but I can say in my defence that the thing was given to me, and hardly anyone knows my number.' 'Then you must know who was trying to call you.' 'Pretty much,' said Loos, 'but back to our theme. You know, my wife travelled once or twice a year to England to visit a friend, the daughter of the family she was an au pair with when she was nineteen. And since she never told me very much about these visits, one day a suspicion crept over me that was otherwise very untypical of me. I asked her in a pseudo-jovial tone whether this friend really existed, or was *she* after all a *he*? She turned very pale. She was quiet so long that I must have gone pale too, since I thought I had hit the bull's eye. She said eventually that we had never talked about fidelity, and for that reason she had assumed it was self-evident. For her, in any case, fidelity was a need, a silent natural instinct, requiring as little strain as love itself, and as long as love was present, I needn't worry. So there seems to be a kind of fidelity that derives neither from an act of will, as I claimed a few minutes ago, nor from an unconscious decree, as you claimed. And this natural fidelity I then found reassuring, when it should rather make us feel anxious.'

'Why though?' I asked. 'Anyway,' Loos continued, 'there was this English friend, who died in June the year before last. Her death was horrible, and could have been the death of my wife as well. They were both walking together in Hyde Park, when a storm came up with uncanny quickness. They ran towards a group of trees to find shelter from the rain, but my wife's sandal fell off in the process. She went back a few steps, stooped down to get it, and noticed that the strap was torn. Her friend had meanwhile reached the trees, and while she was waving to my wife from about forty metres off to get her to hurry up, she was struck by lightning. She died on the spot right before the eyes of my wife, who herself remained unharmed, outwardly, but had to be taken to the hospital for the evaluation, because her legs would no longer carry her. She called me the same evening. I had difficulty understanding her; she sounded as if somebody was strangling her. The next day I flew to London and spent three days at her bedside. There was no medical finding: the doctors spoke of a temporary lameness caused by shock. She could cry on the second day, and she cried for a long time, first in convulsions, then increasingly freely. When I entered her room on the morning of the third day, she was sitting on a chair and was able to get up and walk over to me. Before she was released, a doctor told us something utterly incredible. The friend's death, it turned out, had been caused by the metal wires in her underwired bra – the metal functioned as a lethal conductor. As the doctor recollected, it was the second death from such a cause that he was familiar with. To my question – what would have happened if my wife had been standing next to her friend at the moment of impact, the doctor said that she was unlikely to have survived. In the taxi on the way to the hotel I held her hand – she seemed hardly to be present. "What is a life still worth," she said suddenly, "that owes itself to a torn sandal strap?" "More than before, perhaps," I said, but decided not to go into an explanation, because I sensed that she was sinking back into herself. Well, that's what happened,' Loos said, 'but unfortunately I don't remember anymore what got me talking about this incident.'

I told him it had to do with his doubt about the existence of the English friend or, more exactly, about his wife's fidelity. And that in passing he had also hinted that her kind of fidelity should have made him feel anxious. How he had meant that remained rather obscure to me, but I was interested to hear the answer. After a certain amount of reflection, Loos said that the problem with natural fidelity, as his wife understood it – namely as a mandatory component of love that accompanied it as long as it lasted – the problem with this kind of fidelity was that it was in truth none at all, or in any case, only a virtual fidelity. It was like courage. If you never put yourself in danger, your courage remained untested and unproven, and therefore unrealised. So too with fidelity: to be real and valuable it required temptation, or better, it required an accomplished act of infidelity. Yes, the person who was faithful in the strictest sense was one who had been unfaithful but kept faith with the affected partner. Which, of course, I as a divorce lawyer must certainly know was as rare as the large, forgiving heart on the other side.

I asked Loos, as he paused for a while and took a sip of wine, 'Would you yourself have had it if it had come to that?' 'What?' he asked. 'The large heart,' I said. 'You seem to be missing my point entirely,' Loos answered. 'In that purely hypothetical case I would not have been able to use my heart at all. If a woman tells me she is faithful to me as long as she loves me, then I would have to interpret an infidelity willy-nilly as a sign of extinguished love, and an extinguished love doesn't give a damn for a forgiving heart, do you understand?' 'Thoroughly,' I said. 'And I also understand now why a natural fidelity, as you call it, would in fact cause anxiety. Would you have rather had a wife whose fidelity had been proven by an infidelity?' 'She was as she was, Mr Clarin, and you would have to live three lives to find a woman of such character, of such delicacy, inner and outer.' 'Wonderful for you,' I said, 'that you struck it rich in your very first life. Not so wonderful for me that you think so little of me.' 'I didn't mean you personally, I'm sorry. I mean men generally, including myself. I wasn't much more than a blind sow – although I don't like the comparison because my wife should be compared with something nobler than a mere acorn.' 'How about a truffle?' I asked. 'That would be much better, but according to what I know of them, pigs have no problem finding truffles by scent, even if they're blind. The figure of speech would lose its meaning even if we made the truffle substitution. And I take the comparison back in any case, even as regards me. After all, if I may say so, didn't my wife for her part often characterise me as a gift to her? And now, what am I now?'

Although I saw from looking at him that Loos had directed this question more to himself than to me, I said that he was like a package that was too tightly tied and seemed not to belong to anyone, so that there was no reason for anyone to find and open it. Loos replied that he had in fact mentioned, just ten minutes previously, that he *had* been ready at times during the last six months to untie himself a bit or to let someone else do it. For example – and this would astonish me – he had answered a personal ad. It had been poetically, not to say schmaltzily, phrased: there was talk of the 'velvet cover of the starry sky' under which she, the woman who placed the ad, hoped 'to meet a mature man. – Your Penelope.' That was how the ad was under-signed, and the pseudonym had spoken to the classical philologist in him and made him so curious that he came – with the help of a bottle of red wine – to write a reply letter, which however, not to awaken undue expectations, he did not sign 'Odysseus.' He did, in any case, work two or three subtle classical references into it. After a few days the woman answered, by telephone. Her voice was a little abrasive, but on the other hand, she was to his astonishment actually named Penelope, Penelope Knödler of all things, which dampened his enthu-siasm somewhat, as did the answer she gave when he asked how he would recognise her in the wine bar they had agreed to meet in. She said, to be exact, that her special distinguishing feature consisted in the fact that she had only one ear on the right side. He had laughed dutifully, she practically hooting. But he could see he was going into too much detail, now he'd get to the point. So they met. She was in her mid-forties, a sales office administrator, and attractive as far as looks go. But she had the irritating habit of constantly defining herself, con-stantly saying what it was her habit to do or not to do. It was not her habit, she said for instance, to place personal ads – she didn't have to do that, since it was an easy thing for her to 'peel a man away' from the counter of any bar she chose, which, however, was not her habit. In short, although he, Loos, suffered a bit under Penelope's habits, he was not disinclined when she invited him home for another small drink. He was an exceptional case, she told him when they entered her apart-ment. She wasn't one of those women who would bring a man home with them after the first date. The bedroom door stood open. He saw an enormous bed and on it an enormous down coverlet with a starry sky pattern. But he would abbreviate: Penelope disappeared into the bathroom at some point and, after a long shower, came out all fragrant. All she had on now was a striped bed shirt with side-slits. She sat down next to him on the sofa, snuggled up to him and said that she was someone who always acted on her instinct. Then she called him her cuddly bear. 'Cuddly Bear must also shower first,' she whispered in his ear – her exact words – and instead of immediately taking his leave, he let himself be steered by light pushes of her hands into the bathroom, where she forced on him a poison-green facecloth of a type he had never seen before. Once alone, he felt sober, regathered his willpower, and decided to make a break for it. When he came out of the bathroom, Penelope was already lying expectantly under the starry sky. He went over to the bed and explained in a friendly voice that he would rather not stay, that it didn't feel right to him. She began to whimper like a small child and dug her fingers into him, or rather the leg of his pants. And then, after he managed as gently as he could to free himself from her grip, she lost all composure and all decency, saying among other things that he was a great prudish old bitch. But the most vulgar thing was what she said to him as he was going out the door: 'You rusty jerk-off!' So pitifully, or brutally, had his foray miscarried, his effort to open himself up.

So Loos spoke, with great seriousness and a doleful voice. I didn't want to hurt his feelings or irritate him, so I had to stifle my laugher a number of times, but by the end I lost control. Loos didn't laugh with me, but he didn't seem injured or angry either. He just looked at me with surprise. I got hold of myself quickly and said that in his place I would not have had to be asked twice. 'I know, I know,' Loos said. 'We're hardly alike, despite the common wisdom that all men are equal where the sixth commandment is concerned.' 'But don't forget,' I said, 'it's the women who take this view, and they must know.' 'Women have gown up with this old wives' tale,' said Loos. 'I know mothers whose own husbands don't fit this image at all, but despite knowing better they still tell their daughters that men only want one thing, and that as indiscriminately and immediately as possible. One might almost be ungallant enough to assume that women only pretend to be horrified by the image of men as randy goats.' 'Bugaboo or secret longing, absurd it is not, Mr Loos. Do you know how often a man thinks of sex each day on average?' 'I've never counted.' 'Maybe you haven't, but a research team has, and they came up with two hundred and six. You're amazed at that, aren't you?' 'Yes,' he said, 'it would be a disturbing finding, if we could take it seriously. If a research team were to require me to make a tick in my notebook every time I thought of sex on a given day, I wouldn't be able to think of anything else – the notebook would be full before noon.' 'I assume,' I said, 'that the experiment is not set up on such a simple basis, but however that may be, how can you speak of old wives' tales when the vast majority of men have had experience with prostitutes, which as everyone knows is only about that one quick thing?' 'In contrast to you,' said Loos, 'I don't see the data as evidence of a male's natural constitution, that is, of his true instinctual nature.' 'What else is it, then?' ' A sign of an uncivilised Eros and sexual barbarity. In all spheres of life, in my opinion, a hasty getting to the point and execution without concern for details signifies a coarsening. Only hesitation is human. What I really mean, then, is that what you take for a natural drive, I see rather as a perversion – what is natural for dogs is not necessarily natural for human beings too.' 'How can a person be so blind, or at least so naïve?' I said. 'May I ask you whether you've ever seen a porn-film?' 'Yes,' said Loos, 'inadvertently. Once, in a hotel room, I inadvertently came upon a pay-TV channel.' 'All right, then,' I said. 'You probably know that it's a blooming branch of the economy, with billions in profit, and that legions of men watch these films, and simply and precisely because they serve a need and show what they want to see, what they instinctively dream of – to whit, a quick, direct and completely uninhibited gratification. If there were no genuine desire for that and no demand for such films, there wouldn't be the gigantic supply of them that there is. Do you really believe that all men who consume these things are perverse?'

Loos looked at the clock, drank, puffed on his cigarette. Then he said, 'Not the slightest thing speaks against it. I already explained yesterday evening – though in vain, as I now see – that what the mass of people think and do gradually becomes the norm, and indeed counts as natural, no matter how pathological, warped, or primitive it is. I'd like to quote a sentence that's stuck with me because it horrified me when I first heard it. It comes from the film in the hotel room I just mentioned, comes from the mouth of a woman, and is or was directed at her performing partner. "You fuck like a machine!" she shouted out to him, and she meant it as praise to spur him on. If *those* are the dreams men and women are really supposed to have, if their real wish is to dispatch each other in such a crude way – then don't we have to call such dreams and wishes perverse?' 'You're a master at finding extreme examples,' I said. 'But, if I may repeat myself, to me it's a matter of the principle. The drive is called a *drive* because it drives us to couple with the object of desire without delay. And without delay means also without moral brakes, without inhibition, without shame. It is a pure desire of nature. In a porn film it breaks forth triumphant; that's what makes it so stimulating.'

'I have a desire of nature too,' said Loos. 'My glass is empty. Shall we order another carafe?' 'Without delay,' I said. 'Only it's going to be critical again for my use of the car.' 'If necessary we'll walk again,' he said. And continued suddenly, 'When I was an adolescent it only took a plain bra ad in a black-and-white magazine to make my ears burn and to nurse my fantasy. I didn't ask for stronger stimuli or go looking for them. But over the years more and more was shown. More suggestive images were supplied, whether there was a demand for them or not – and of course people looked at them. And then they got used to the sight, which in turn increased the appetite of many of them for more explicit fare. And at the culmination stands pornography as the supposed maximal stimulus. At the culmination of the subtle process of directing our needs and training our eyes and taste, the suppliers boldly claim they have been guided solely by the demand and genuine desires of their customers. The tabloid owners and television bosses justify the monstrous garbage they feed the masses in the same mendaciously criminal way. First they mould people's tastes to tastelessness and promote simple-mindedness, then they appeal to the result and the needs of their supposedly adult customers. Am I right or am I right?'

'Neither right nor wrong, I'm afraid,' I said. 'The argument over the chicken and the egg is of course as fascinating as ever, but we're hardly likely to settle it. I do wonder about one thing, though. If people are as easily moulded and directed as you regard them to be, why only to the negative, why only in the direction of bad taste, indiscriminateness, primitiveness on all levels? If the masses are so happy to have their minds made up for them, we should be able to bring them to recognise garbage as garbage and to become receptive to more refined fare, which – if desired on a broad scale – would be just as profitable. Of course, this will never happen. It remains the case that the more primitive the newspaper, the higher the circulation; the dumber the broadcast, the higher the ratings. The only question is why it is so, and with all due respect, your answer doesn't convince me.' 'Nor me, entirely,' said Loos, 'yet it's still better than yours, in any case more pleasant. For you, man comes into the world already a moron, or at least with an instinctive inclination to the moronic. As a pedagogue, I can't afford that view, not before retirement. No, let me correct myself. It's not a matter of not being able to afford it: I would also have little right to adopt it on the basis of my experience. As a teacher, that is, it has now and then struck me how strong a will we have to make ourselves smarter, how much of an interest in things new and challenging. The appetite for thinking and knowing is there, even if you can't always count on it. I'm talking about the students, of course, and less about the rest.' 'I assume the "rest" are your colleagues?' Loos nodded and paused for a while.

He was in the bloom of youth when he started teaching, he then said, and the older, and old, colleagues of that time were now either dead or in nursing homes and other institutions, where they presumably sat in diapers vegetating their lives away with Alzheimer's disease or strokes. And yet it seemed only yesterday that these same colleagues, with few exceptions, had been acting like gods, delivering cutting remarks in those interminable conferences that had to do, among other things, with the question of promoting or holding students back, or with the review of the grades the teachers had turned in. 'My grades cannot be altered!' most of the queried teachers had more bellowed than said – they had entered them in the transcript up to three places after the decimal point and therefore regarded them as extremely precise and irrevocable. And all these narrow-minded bigots, these fate-impersonating, course-of-life-determining judges, if they were still alive, were now dozing their lives away in dementia, just as the politicians and the other erstwhile agitators and loudmouths were today either dead or gone to ruin. Just a short while ago, he, Loos, had witnessed a chilling sight with his own eyes, right in the long corridor of the nursing home where his mother lived. A dwarfish little man came shuffling toward him, pulling a pine cone behind him attached to a three-yard length of string, and this old greybeard was in fact none other than his former English teacher, a petulant and repulsive swine, whom everyone hated and feared. In short, it must be a consolation and satisfaction to the victims of these high and mighty scandals-to-their-profession to learn about their deaths or reduction to idiocy, though the wounds did not thereby heal any faster. Besides, he, Loos, was not without guilt, he had occasionally hurt students' feelings and failed to do them justice, but since his offences were not intentional, his former charges would possibly be satisfied with his dripping nose and hearing aid and not want to see him suffering harsher punishments when they met him on the street. 'But now, Mr Clarin, I notice once again how erratic and undisciplined my talk has become – once more I've drifted off topic, from Penelope for example, about whom I'd still like to add a short word.

'Naturally you think that I fled from her because the ghost of my wife wanted it so, and perhaps too because you think I have a weak sexual drive. I don't think either one is accurate – the latter more probable, but only if you want to characterise as weak a drive that demands something more than a fragrant body. It was a question of this *more* – it was missing, and that lack would have turned coitus into rape, that is, into a mechanical performance, even though Penelope would have welcomed it. I know that people can reduce each other, mutually and in the lack of emotional ties, to their mere sex, but that only brings more sadness than bliss. Therefore I would also have sexually abused myself if I had heeded Penelope's appeal to join her under the starry coverlet. Don't misunderstand me, I felt like doing it, but I felt something else too, something that proved stronger and accordingly determined what I did – this was the feeling of a missing togetherness, of an incompatible chemistry of souls. And so on and so forth – I resent your nodding! It makes me orate all the more. I'm going up to my room for a minute.'

I was glad for the pause, glad to be released for a few minutes from the oppressive presence of this man. But I never for a second wished he would stay upstairs and leave me sitting there. I wondered whether my interest in other people had always in truth been lukewarm or only *appeared* lukewarm now, measured against the powerful interest that Loos aroused in me. I couldn't tell. I wondered how his wife had been able to stand this in every respect difficult man. I tried to stop wondering and relax. When Loos still wasn't back after ten minutes, I noticed that my fingers were restless, as if I were going through withdrawal. Loos took upon himself the right to make me wait. I cursed him inwardly as a blustering half-geezer. It was now five past ten. If he wasn't back in three minutes, I would just leave. When the three minutes went by, I gave him another three. He came just before ten thirty. I felt relieved.

He sat down and said, 'It's all fog, the lights across the way aren't visible. I stood at the window like a blind man, and the futility of looking helped me realise that a thinking being isn't dependent on its eyes. A simple recognition sometimes takes time to dawn on us, doesn't it? And incidentally, it isn't really true that it was your nodding that led me to orate. You actually nod very seldom. I think I've already given you a picture here and there of how things stand with me: along with my wife I also lost my speech, or at least the companionability to which speech belongs and in which it plays the chief role. I've withdrawn, even from friends, and have practically stopped talking, certainly about anything private. My vocal chords would be mildewed if I didn't have school to force me to speak. When you sat down at my table yesterday evening, I'm sorry, but I was worried that you might speak to me, so much so that I wished I had a magic hood to make me disappear and not have to talk to you. But you're a fowler, and an able one at that. You lured me out of the bush, caught me, and made me so tame that I started twittering with the obsessive zeal of a bird that has been silent the whole winter. So much for an explanation of my communication compulsion. I ask your indulgence.'

'I'm the one who should be asking for indulgence,' I said. 'I pushed myself on you and disturbed your privacy. It's very easy for me to initiate contact, and as an extroverted person I clearly run the risk of sometimes not noticing that others are different. I feel comfortable with people and don't like being alone. Unsociability isn't in my vocabulary. It's a riddle to me how people live and let live without social intercourse. Good, you luckily still have the school. But what do you do in your free time? What do you do during vacations? Do you at least travel sometimes?' 'I hold with Ovid,' said Loos, '*bene qui latuit, bene vixit*.' 'You'll have to translate that for me,' I said. 'I'm afraid I only understand the *bene*. Latin was never my forte.' '"One who has hidden well, has lived well,"' said Loos, 'but the pack animal can hardly imagine that kind of wisdom. And incidentally, I'm not so terribly alone, I have inner company, but never mind that. You'd be amazed: I do what I've had in mind since birth; namely nothing. I don't always succeed at it, of course, but I keep practising and I'm on my way. "The wise man yields," I say to myself and leave it to the doers to struggle against the law of gravity.' 'What does doing nothing look like exactly, and how can you practise it?' I asked Loos. 'Well,' he said, 'in this as in everything else: keep trying over and over, till you succeed.

Say that you lie down on the sofa on Saturday at noon and set yourself the task of lying there for two hours, at rest, but without sleeping. You hear a neighbour vacuuming or someone mowing a lawn, but instead of thinking about things you have to do, you should just watch the spider that squats motionless on your ceiling and on no account yield to the urge to get rid of it. Now the telephone rings. As a beginner you jump up and reach for the receiver. That would only be alarming if you learned nothing from your failure. Go back into yourself and practise more, until you've achieved the freedom of no longer reacting to external stimuli, which try to betray you into doing something.'

'I understand,' I said, 'but what is it all for, where is the sense in the practice?' 'Maybe,' Loos said, 'you would experience for two hours what it feels like not to be a slave, how peaceful it is inside yourself when you lose for a time that constant feeling that you have to be doing something.' 'To each his own,' I answered. 'I'm more comfortable when I'm active, even when there's a *must* behind my activity and not a personal *will*.' 'Yes, yes,' Loos said, '"Of idleness comes no goodness," as the saying goes. I said it to myself, no, hammered it in, to persuade myself to fly to Zakynthos. You asked me about any trips I might have taken, didn't you? I took one, eight days last year in Zakynthos, and the pomposity of the saying proved itself a scandal. My vacation was shit. I use the word deliberately, it's the only vulgar word I ever heard from my wife's mouth, and that only once. She never cursed, you see, and she hardly ever used strong language – but you'd be wrong to think she was prudish or staid, she was just refined, and if it didn't sound so madonna-like, I'd say *pure*. She stood one morning before the bedroom mirror, naked, and probably thought the door to the room I was sitting in was closed and I couldn't hear her. As you know there are areas on a woman's body that count as problem zones, because they're especially susceptible to fat. Even my wife was a little fuller here and there than she had been, and she hated these areas, whereas I was fond of them. She didn't believe me, though I tried to convince her. She found it unpleasant to be touched in such a place. She would really shrink back. But to be brief: she stood one morning in front of the bedroom mirror and said fairly loud, "I look like shit!"'

Loos looked past me, absently, as if he were listening for her words.

When he seemed present again – I saw it by the fact that he took out his handkerchief to wipe away a few small trickles of sweat that were running towards his eyebrows – I reminded him of Zakynthos and asked why he hadn't enjoyed his vacation there. The onerous part of it, he said, had already begun on the flight over there, when the woman who sat beside him pestered him with the details of her private life. She had recently been divorced after twenty-one years of marriage, she told him, and now she was about to learn how to let go and grow inwardly with new experience. Et cetera. Didn't he too think that every ending was at the same time a new beginning and accordingly brought with it an opportunity to forge ahead to new horizons and people? Et cetera. He, Loos, had said as little as possible, in the hope that the torrent would trickle out, but the ploy was unsuccessful. There are people who have no feel for distance, no inner feel and sometimes not even an outer one. When you stand talking to such people, they keep stepping closer to you, and as soon as you step back to regain the necessary foot-and-a-half distance, they shorten it with another step forward to about half that. He had a colleague who in every conversation pushed him backwards several yards through the teachers' lounge. But however that may be – after their arrival in Zakynthos he lost sight of the woman and climbed exhausted into a taxi that the hotel had sent to pick him up. The driver said he needed another person staying in the same hotel to make the drive. After a fairly long wait a thin woman got in and brought him new suffering when she started getting personal and talking about her divorce as soon as the cab got underway. He was now virtually sure that the travel agency had kept him in the dark about the target groups that travel to Zakynthos. The woman tortured him further with two or three foot operations and acquainted him with the fact that she had been an official with the criminal investigation department of the police before her early retirement. When they got to the hotel, there was a hassle. He had booked a double room with balcony and sea-view, well knowing what kind of dingy cells hotels typically stick lone travellers in. To such a room they had now in fact assigned him, and it was only thanks to his stiffest resistance that justice prevailed in the end. He then reconnoitered the village, which according to the travel brochure was a quiet fishing village, but was in reality only one long, noisy street with innumerable taverns, discos and bars. That evening he sat on his double bed and asked himself why he had come. He felt his presence there superfluous and at the same time realised that it was the superfluousness of his being at home that had driven him there. During the night dogs howled for hours, and in the morning, after breakfast, the police official suddenly stood before him, screamed hello, and sat down gabbing at his table. The horror repeated itself in the evening. He had taken a seat in one of the taverns, outside of course, and felt relaxed for the first time – even if a little annoyed by the eternal Zorba music and the body-lotion smells from the mostly silent couples around him. When he saw her coming, the police official, he dropped his napkin and dived under the table to hide, but she, the official, was already standing in front of him when he surfaced. At least this time she asked whether she could join him. Instead of a *no*, he uttered a *please*, and in so doing detested his parents, for nothing was harder to shed than good breeding.

Loos drank, fixing me the while with his gaze, and asked whether his twaddle interested me at all and whether, if it didn't, I had the courage to say so. I answered truthfully that it did interest me, he shouldn't worry, and should just go on with the story. 'Good,' said Loos, 'but I'll try anyway not to get lost. And lest I seem a misogynist, let me just say that the official from Bern was not only unattractive, but devoid of any subtlety of feeling. Her speech was coarse, her voice loud, and her talk mere blather. She might have compensated for this a bit by telling me about some fascinating criminal case, but that never happened. When I asked about something of the sort she just said that she had worked in the office and had little to do with the frontlines. But she seemed to have an instinct for it, because in the coming days she succeeded in tracking me down almost everywhere I was. When I found a chair on the beach that was surrounded right, left, front, and back by other occupied chairs, I admit I felt hemmed in, but at least I was protected from her. So I sometimes eluded her detection, but could never calmly enjoy it. I simply sat on the chair, occasionally pawing the sand with my feet, and my disconsolate mood was brightened only by the thought that all the bodies around me would one day turn to dust. I retreated more and more to my room, or rather to my balcony, but it soon became evident that the balcony wouldn't work either. If I sat there in the afternoon, I saw down below various topless women in the sand, some sitting, some lying, and sometimes one would look up and nudge another, who would likewise look up, and it wasn't hard to guess from their giggling what they took me for. So the balcony was out – it wasn't even granted me to sit there in peace late in the evening and drink an ouzo, because on the next balcony two German couples were playing a game, some card game I think, that seemed to involve somebody constantly saying "mau" or "maumau" – all I heard for hours was mau and maumau either spoken or screamed. The vacation wore me down, and I take it that the dream I had the night before I left, of which I remember only the chief image, was trying to express symbolically the sum value of my Zakynthos days. In this dream I saw myself in a grotesque form, namely as a gnawed bone – not a skeleton, understand, but a bone all of one piece that had two protuberances on the lower end that it could hop on, but only backwards. Curious, no? That I, a heavy-set man, see myself as a bone of all things! Maybe the dream image was also simply trying to tell me I should stop stuffing myself. You should know that after the loss of my wife I put on about seventeen pounds. I had no desire to drink wine any more, instead I ate too much and got heavier than I should. It embarrasses me somewhat to talk about this craving, partly because of the saying that stupid people eat while the smart ones drink. Do you remember the storm?'

'Last night's storm? Of course. What makes you think of that?' 'I'm sorry,' said Loos, 'I mean the storm in Hyde Park, the fatal lightning bolt. I wanted to say that my wife changed after this body blow, and one of the signs of it was eating sweets. She did it secretly and in considerable quantities. I came upon it by accident. Knowing my fondness for good pencils she had given me a brass pencil sharpener, and one day as I was bent over the waste basket in the kitchen about to sharpen a pencil, the sharpener fell out of my hand. It disappeared so completely in the trash that I had to empty the basket and fill it again, and in so doing I found a huge number of crumpled chocolate-wrappers. This discovery stirred me somehow, and it also made me sad to see my wife hiding things from me. She must have known that I wouldn't have begrudged her all the sweets she could eat. Naturally I said nothing. I in no way wanted her to feel guilty, like a child caught stealing cookies. I also said nothing about a slip of paper I found poking through the trash, although I would have liked to know the meaning of the sentence she had scribbled down on it: "I want no sky that sticks to the windowpane." A strange image, isn't it? So my wife changed a little after the accident in Hyde Park. The most understandable part of it for me was the fact that, although she never had any problem with storms before, now she began to sweat and tremble at even distant thunder and sheet lightning. And unfortunately I couldn't calm her down and take her in my arms, because in these moments of anxiety she also feared being touched, so that it almost seemed to me as if she saw me as a part of what threatened her. Afterwards she would feel guilty and let herself be consoled. And once, she told me that she could no longer ride the elevator with her mother, who lived on the sixth floor of an apartment building, without being attacked by anxiety over her mother's proximity. Certain of her idiosyncrasies and sensitivities had always been there, admittedly, and only became more pronounced after the experience in London. Her body, I should tell you, was a virtual divining rod that reacted to every imaginable source of disturbance in the most sensitive way. In the early years of our marriage, we moved twice within the greater Zurich area, and in each place changed the position of the bed several times because my wife felt, on one occasion, the harmful effects of underground watercourses and, another time, low-frequency magnetic fields. Foehns and full moons also oppressed her. But for all that, you'd have a false impression of my wife if you thought of her as sickly, whining or neurasthenic. She was sensitive rather than neurasthenic, and that she was no whiner God knows she later proved beyond all doubt when she really was sick and had to deal with the worst. My memory fails me, did I tell you about this yesterday? I mean about her sickness?'

'You spoke of a tumour, but only hintingly. You said also that the tumour was successfully operated on and that her blonde hair, that was shaved for the surgery, grew back quickly.' 'Bravo!' said Loos. 'You'd make a gifted liar.' 'Where do you get that? I don't know what you mean.' 'Just a joke,' said Loos, 'just a reference to Quintilian, who thinks that liars require an excellent memory. To cut a long story short, about ten months after the event in Hyde Park, my wife began to suffer from nocturnal headaches. And sometimes even before breakfast she had to throw up. Only the last I took seriously. I insisted she have a pregnancy test and hoped for a child. But there was nothing in it – the door remained closed to the late fulfilment of that hope. One morning my wife said to me that I looked distorted to her. I immediately called her in sick, despite her resistance. I've probably already mentioned that she worked in a jewellery factory where she superintended the wedding ring section. This by the by. When she then felt numb in the left half of her body, she went to the doctor. He had tests done immediately. The diagnosis came quickly and with it my horror. Astrocytoma. A swelling of the star-shaped supporting cells in the brain. My wife stayed eerily calm, so that I thought she underestimated the danger she was in. She had a piano tuner come as if that were now the most urgent thing to do. Two days later when I came home from the school – my wife was still at the doctor's – I listened to the answering machine and heard the voice of the young, blonde piano tuner, Rossi was his name, saying, "Mrs Loos, I'd love to kiss your legs". That's all he said. I was embarrassed, though also concerned. The twerp must have sensed something in my wife's manner that encouraged his audacity. Yet my wife in her behaviour with other men was extremely reserved, dismissive almost; I have never been able to detect her sending subtle flirting signals the way most women do. So I was concerned, because I had once read that brain tumours can also lead to personality changes, and something like that seemed to be at work here, if my wife had indeed given the young man any sign of encouragement. I told her when she got home that there was a message for her on the machine. She listened to it and laughed long and heartily. But wasn't she shocked, I asked. Shouldn't somebody give this kid a good dressing down? "Don't be silly!" she said. "You know, a little while ago I would still have found his advance outrageous, but now it seems harmless and sweet, and even funny. The MRI of my brain forces me to think of my approaching end. And strangely, everything, or almost everything, that I now relate to that end or try to see from its vantage comes across as somehow funny, do you know what I mean? – it loses its weight." When I let her know that I did know what she meant, she said something that I didn't understand and still don't understand today. She said that she had often wished, in vain, not to be understood by me. I asked her to explain what she said, but she refused. But to return to the point: I actually only wanted to say that my wife, contrary to my suspicions, certainly did not mistake the gravity of her situation. And in fact she stayed cheerful while I myself nearly lost my mind with anxiety, worry and helplessness. She consoled me instead of vice versa. She told me, for instance, she had heard a radio programme a while back about an ancient people and their strange custom of greeting newborns with lamentation and enumerating all the evils that awaited them. They buried their dead, however, with jubilation and banter, because they had finally escaped the sufferings of life. Didn't I like this custom too? my wife asked. I didn't mention that I was familiar with the Thracians' custom and said, "Yes, in a way, but nevertheless the idea of a dance of jubilation around my grave makes me a little melancholy." "Not me," she said, "It would make me glad to see you dance." "You will experience it," I said to her. "As soon as you get better, I'll do a dance." "With me?" she asked. "With you," I said.

'Yet we didn't dance then,' said Loos. 'We only danced once with each other, at our wedding party, then never again. I took a dance course when I was seventeen, and that first evening a girl who smelled of lavender soap told me that I shouldn't hop around so much. At the end of the third evening came the so-called ladies' choice. I waited in vain to be chosen, remaining superfluously in my seat. I felt like a stunted calf at a cattle market. It was out of the question that I would ever find a girlfriend, let alone a wife. I didn't finish the dance course and didn't dance again till my wedding, and even then only very briefly and self-ironically, so to speak. She could go dancing anytime she felt like it, I used to tell her sometimes, but she always said that dancing didn't matter to her. And yet when I met her, I had even thought she might possibly be a ballerina, because she looked like one with her graceful figure. A ballerina with a dog, who was walking toward me on a dirt path through a field. I too, exceptionally, had a dog with me, the dachshund of my landlady, who had asked me to take care of it for two days because she wanted to travel to Alsace. The dog was actually a bitch, named Lara, and in heat. For that reason the landlady had also given me a special deterrent spray as well as instructions to spray a cloud of it over her hind-parts before going out on walks. This seemed exaggerated to me, as well as disagreeable, and so I avoided doing it, an avoidance that proved fateful. It was a bright evening in March, and Lara trotted on ahead of me – I had freed her from the leash. So then, a young woman was approaching from the opposite direction with a Labrador retriever. When we were still about twenty yards apart, Lara stopped still. The Labrador, who was on the leash, likewise stopped still. And then everything happened very fast. The Labrador tore himself loose with a jerk and stormed over to Lara. "Leo, Leo!" called my future wife, but Leo was no longer accessible to address, he was already intensely sniffing, and Lara signalled her consent by laying her tail to the side, whereupon he mounted her immediately. It was too late for any intervention. Confused and embarrassed – united in shame, I might say – we both stood to the side and, apart from a few commonplace apologies, didn't know what to say to each other. But now there was a complication which, as I've been told, is not all that rare: the male, after the successful copulation, was trying vainly to dismount, but remained stuck in Lara as if in a vice. For a short while the two wedged-together animals turned noiselessly in a circle. Then Leo put one of his hind legs up on Lara's back and twisted his body off and around, so that the two, still welded together, now stood hinterpart to hinterpart. Then each of them, yelping with pain, started to pull in the opposite direction. In vain – they couldn't pry themselves loose from each other. It was an unsettling drama. The young woman blushed in waves, and I could find no words to release the tension. After a quarter of an hour, the longest of my life, my wife-to-be declared that we had to do something, or the drama would never end. 'Yes, but what?' I asked, and instead of answering she approached Leo from the front – he wasn't big or heavy – grabbed him around the flanks with both hands, lifted him up a little bit, and pulled on him with a slight twisting motion. The grip seemed to loosen, the separation succeeded, and both animals began licking their genitals. And that's how we made our acquaintance. Unthinkable what might have happened if I had reached for the spray as I should have done before the walk – namely, nothing. We would have walked by and greeted each other on the dirt path, and Leo would have sniffed at Lara briefly, if at all, turned away with a shudder, and then, yanking energetically at the leash, pulled the love of my life out of my field of vision forever. Thank God it happened otherwise. Thank God the young woman didn't simply leave after the incident, but was concerned about the outcome. "We can only hope now," she said, "that the act of nature has no consequences." "Act of nature!" – that's what she really said, that sticks in the memory, and it was immediately clear to me: "If a young women of this sort calls the generative process an act of nature, she must be a special person."

I asked her whether I should let her know about the possible conse-quences. She begged me to do so and gave me her telephone number. She told me her name, I told her mine, her handshake was pleasant. I can't speak of love at first sight – I've never been easily inflammable. We began to meet regularly, once we started, and only gradually fell in love – and it would now be time for me to keep quiet for a while and give myself the chance to prove myself as good a listener as you, Mr Clarin. Talk! Tell me about yourself. For heavens sake, reveal some-thing about yourself too for a change!'

He doesn't let me get a word in, I might have thought, he talks himself to a fever pitch and then reproaches me for being silent. But I didn't think that, I didn't feel it that way. I recalled my mother who often read to me when I was a child from Grimms' fairy tales. I used to listen – all caught up in them, enraptured. How terribly, I now realised, this capacity is impaired in the course of time. I realised this, because the capacity was suddenly there again as if newly awakened by the powerful presence of Loos telling his stories. I hadn't had the desire to take the initiative, although I otherwise like to talk and don't feel at all uncomfortable, in groups of people like myself, taking the role of the alpha male who dominates the conversation. But now, as I said, I felt no need to talk, probably also because I was afraid of disappoint-ing Loos's unexpected interest. He seemed to have brought me to the point of finding myself and my life almost insipid. He was looking at me. 'In your place I would have lost patience with me long ago,' he said. Someone who's gripped, I responded, needed no patience. What did demand my patience somewhat was the fact that he hardly ever told a story to the end and so even with Lara he left me uncertain whether she got pregnant or not. 'It's true, I never conclude things,' said Loos, 'and Lara unfortunately did not get pregnant.' 'Why unfortunately?' I asked. 'That I don't want to say right now,' he said. 'You have the floor.' It wasn't easy to speak on demand, I said, and besides I didn't know what he wanted to hear from me. Loos filled our glasses. 'I would also like to suggest we drop the formalities,' he said. 'It isn't necessary anymore for us to keep to a distance with *Mister* and the like.' Loos's proposal came so unexpectedly that I couldn't react immediately. 'We don't have to,' he said, 'it was just an impulse.' 'No, I'm very glad of it,' I said quickly, although it wasn't quite true. In truth I was happy with the distance he now wanted to remove. His gravitational field, if I can use that term, already exercised a strong enough pull on me. 'I'm Thomas,' I said. Loos started for a second and then said, 'I suspected that.' 'Suspected? But why?' 'Well,' he said, 'last night I saw the name-plate on your door: *T Clarin*, and on the way back I was trying to come up with all the first names that begin with a T. I only found eight, and Thomas seemed to me to fit you the best. Incidentally something binds us: my name is the same as yours.' 'Thomas?' 'Thomas, yes.'

Before I could say anything about this coincidence, Loos said that something else had struck him on the way home. My nameplate, together with a second, was located on the left doorframe. And on the right frame he had seen a third plate, made of brass and discoloured with verdigris, but still legible. As I knew, it read *Tasso*, and this celebrated name had very much surprised him. 'You are a riddle to me, Mr – I mean, Thomas,' I said. 'How can you drink as much as you did yesterday and yet be so sharp-sighted?' His size allowed him much, he said, but did I not want to tell him who this Tasso was? 'He was my best friend,' I said. 'As students we lived in rooms that shared a common wall. He's not alive anymore. The house in Agra belonged to him, he died there at age twenty-six.'

'In contrast to me, you know how to say things concisely,' said Loos, 'only there's no meat on the bone. More meat, Thomas, if I may ask! Was this Tasso possibly a relative of the famous mad poet?' 'He was often asked that,' I said, 'and he used to say modestly that he didn't know. He came from the area around Naples, and when he was five years old, he lost both parents in a car accident. He was transplanted to Switzerland, to Bern, where his father's sister lived. She was married without children to a Swiss engineer named Engel, who when Tasso was thirteen fell into an elevator shaft. He left his wife a considerable fortune as well as a cottage in Agra, where she moved when Tasso started at the university. Two years later, she also died, with cancer of the lymph nodes I believe, and the cottage passed into Tasso's possession. Is that all right, Thomas, or shall I rein in more?' 'There's too much dying,' said Loos, 'otherwise it's fine. Tell on!' 'Good, then. When I started at the university, I found a small, cheap room in the loft of a stately old house that belonged to a baker's widow. I had to share the bathroom with the tenants of two other rooms, and one of them was the still unknown to me Tasso. He had already been living there for some time – he was in his fourth semester, studying History and English – and the fact that we became close friends borders on a miracle. He was the exact opposite of me, outwardly certainly, but I'm talking about our respective natures. Everything that's associated with the south – lightheartedness, nonchalance, gregariousness, loquacity, perhaps even superficiality – all of this was really my trademark, whereas Tasso was serious and phlegmatic, conscientious and thorough. He had what I lacked and vice versa. You can imagine how interesting, but also how full of tension, our friendship was. We were so intimate that we could admit to each other our occasional feelings of antipathy for each other. For instance, I was always planning to get up earlier in the morning than he did for once, but I never managed it and resented him for my defeat. Only much later did I become an early riser and learn to discipline myself. Giovanni's antipathy – that was his name – was related to my love life or rather, as he put it, my compulsory "consumption of women," which naturally affected him since we shared a wall. But it wasn't the noises, he said, that sparked resentment in him, nor was it envy, but rather the fact that my fickle behaviour made him feel sorry for the women. In his opinion they didn't deserve, nor could they handle, being treated so dismissively, and he meant *dismissively* literally, he said. But in spite of all differences our friendship was never endangered. One time he knocked on my door long after midnight and called in a low voice asking if I was still awake. 'Somewhat,' I said, 'come in.' He held a book in his hands and said shyly that he had found a sentence in it that related to us, and it was this: "Be to your friend an uncomfortable pillow." At that I leapt out of bed and uncorked a Chianti, and our friendship was now defined, so to speak.'

'Wrong,' said Loos. 'Nietzsche said "a hard field-cot" and not "an uncomfortable pillow."' 'I thank you humbly for the correction,' I said, 'but the sense is exactly the same.' 'Excuse me,' he said, 'the philologist in me has taken over.' 'Never mind,' I said. 'However that may be, a little later Tasso fell in love, for the first time actually, and as hopelessly hard as only late starters can. In any case, he spoke now only of marriage, although he confided to me at the same time that he found kissing a lot less easy than it looked in the movies. He also told me that the only reason he hadn't yet introduced Magdalena to me was his anxiety about the mockingly evaluative look I gave women. I promised him I would look at her as if she were a flower. But then the first time I saw her, I forgot about the flower and saw only the woman, and understood why Tasso was so entranced. And as much as I saw that there was something about her that my girlfriends didn't have, that something remained obscure to me. I only sensed that I would never have got anywhere with Magdalena even if she had been free. Nevertheless, I found her immediately congenial, and since I also thought I saw how well they suited each other, I gave up on the idea of putting the breaks on Tasso and rubbing his nose in everything he'd be missing if he married his first love. He had never wanted to hear it and once explained with embarrassment that the only thing that occasionally put the brakes on him was his worry that he might not be equal to Magdalena's physical desires. As I certainly knew, yet couldn't understand – he said – he was, despite his more than twenty-five years, virtually clueless in this regard, whereas Magdalena had already had experience. And so he was afraid that she would find him wanting and possibly even regard him as a bungler, which, he said, he certainly was. Did that mean he hadn't yet slept with her, I asked. He said that for him kissing was miracle enough, he didn't want to rush the rest. "My God," I said, "you rush into marriage, but the screwing can wait?!" "It's true," he said.

'That was in the spring, and the wedding took place in the summer. They travelled down to Ticino and spent two weeks in his house. Then Magdalena went back – she worked as a speech therapist – while Giovanni stayed, in order to write his degree papers without distraction. They called each other daily, and she visited him at the weekends. At the end of August she called me, on a Wednesday. She said she had left Agra on Sunday evening and since then had heard nothing more from Tasso and couldn't reach him herself. She asked whether he had called me. No, I said and reassured her. I even laughed at her: it seemed to me really overdoing it to be alarmed after just two and a half days of telephone silence. But she was alarmed, and when she heard nothing from Giovanni on Thursday either, she got on the train on Friday. What she discovered in Tasso's house is beyond the bounds of imagination. It was so unspeakably horrible that she lost consciousness for a little while. He lay curled up on the sofa, with ants and swarms of flies all over him.'

I paused and drank. 'Gruesome,' murmured Loos. 'Murder or suicide?' 'Neither,' I said. 'He died a natural death, as was conclusively established: heart attack, sudden cardiac death, probably already on Monday and probably caused by a genetic defect of the cardiac valve. It is certain that he did not suffer, that was the only consolation. Magdalena weathered it all, but then, weeks after Tasso was buried, she had to experience something that made her collapse altogether. Tasso had the habit of almost always carrying a camera with him, a small compact one that he called his little notebook. I seldom saw the photos he took. They were distinguished by their lack of anything distinctive about them. He had a weakness and an eye for the nondescript. To get to the point: there was still film in his camera and Magdalena had it developed in order to know, as she said, what had caught Tasso's eye in the last days or hours of his life. The exposure counter indicated that seven pictures had been taken, and seven developed pictures came back. They all showed a naked woman, some from the front, some from the back, lying on the sofa with the bright blue throw-cloth, the same one on which Tasso had lain when Magdalena found him.'

Loos stared at me. I was quiet. 'Go on,' he said with a strangely hoarse voice. 'How go on?' I said. 'I've told the whole story.' 'No,' said Loos, 'there's never a whole story, never a conclusion, just arbitrary breaking off where one likes. Who was this woman?' 'We don't know. Magdalena cut out just the head from one the photos that showed her face and showed it to everyone who was close to Tasso. No one had ever seen the woman, and no one could believe that Tasso was capable of leading a double life. Magdalena looked through his things in vain for some indication, trying to come to some conclusion, but there wasn't the least scrap of evidence. But I forgot to mention that the date the photos were taken was printed on the back – it was three days before Magdalena's last visit, I mean the last weekend they spent together. I have no other explanation than that my friend, once he was sexually awakened, lost control of his drives – he couldn't contain himself and paid a prostitute to make a house visit. Of course that doesn't fit the person we knew, but I have no other interpretation, because one thing for me is dead certain: Tasso as lover had no mistress.'

'What did she look like, this woman?' Loos asked. 'Hard to say. I didn't see the pictures, only the cutout of the face, which had something Slavic about it, prominent cheekbones, reddish blonde hair, features on the rough side: a mature woman – she had to be at least ten years older than Tasso. Why do you ask?' 'No particular reason, Mr Clarin,' said Loos. 'Go on.' 'I can only add,' I said, with added irritation because Loos had used my last name again, 'I can only add that Magdalena, with the help of therapy, gradually emerged from the crippling depression that overtook her after the double trauma. She never wanted to enter the house in Agra again and sold it four years ago to a colleague, my partner in the law practice, and me. And that's it.'

'Naturally it's not easy to live with an abyss,' Loos said, 'and there's a great temptation to try to sound it to its depths. We shouldn't – it leads only to angry grief. If we look down into it, straining our ears, we hear the sound of our own gnashing teeth or their echo, nothing more. "Who are you? What does it look like in your inmost self?"

Futile questions, vain importunity. And in spite of this, in spite of this, I know Tasso, even if I was not his best friend, as you were.' 'I don't follow,' I said. 'Are you bent on confusing me? Did you know Tasso?' 'You make it easy for me to listen to you,' he said. 'The tragic suits me – only, it's embarrassing – my bladder. Mind if I ask for another short intermission?' I watched him go and resolved never to become so cranky and eccentric.

When he came back, he said, 'The fog is pulling back, and the sky is clearing. I can see the lights. Maybe we can hope for a bright Pentecost Sunday. And as I mentioned earlier, even the minds of the people closest to us are sealed with seven seals. What I know about Tasso, I know from you, and yet, in the matter of this mysterious woman, I get a different picture than you, because I assess the details differently. Forget the breach in the dam. Forget the excess of impatience and sexual hunger. Connect Tasso's great love with his inexperience in the physical domain, and recall his touching anxiety about disappointing his beloved and lacking expertise as a man with her. Imagine him reading a newspaper and coming upon an ad that says something like "Mature, affectionate woman makes house and hotel-room visits." It's a temptation for Tasso, but specifically the temptation of paying for a short course in love. He has the woman come, and now I have to speculate: he realises, when she arrives, that he had misjudged himself for a second. He doesn't want another woman, not even for practice – he can't do that. She takes her clothes off unasked, lies on the sofa, and whispers "come here" in Italian. He stands there awkwardly for a while, until an idea strikes him. He doesn't want anything more, he says, than to take a few pictures. "One of those, are you?" she says. And that he can cheerfully manage.'

I didn't doubt for a second that Loos had lifted the veil, that his reconstruction and interpretation were right. I hated him. I hated him because he forced me to slap my forehead and admit that I was blind as a bat about Tasso's motives. I also felt something like jealousy, as if Loos had taken possession of my best friend, stolen him from me posthumously. 'You're right to knit your brows, Thomas,' said Loos. 'I could be wrong. Don't tell Magdalena about my theory. She'd convince herself it was true and fall into a double distress after a year and a day. She'd probably see in retrospect that she had painfully come to terms with something that was not at all what she thought it was. Then she'd have feelings of shame and guilt about the dead Tasso because she had failed to believe in him despite the bad light he appeared in. How is she now?' 'Really well. She's married again and just recently became a mother.'

'And how's the other woman?' 'What other woman?' 'The one with the nerve problems, the one you once ate with here.' 'Oh her,' I said. 'I have no idea. We haven't seen each other since the break-up. How do you come to mention her?' 'Very indirectly,' Loos said. 'Unless I'm mistaken, she's the only woman besides Magdalena who, as far as I can tell, has played a role in your life – you haven't told me about any other.' 'That just has to do with the place we're in, that reminded me of her. She was no more important to me than others, which isn't to say that I was indifferent to her. By the way, though, I don't think of you as a man who has any interest in flings and affairs.' 'May I know what brings you to this conclusion?' '*You* ask that? The ardent champion of the so-called great love!' 'Thomas,' said Loos, 'love doesn't need to be championed any more than the sun. What has been granted to me, undeservedly, has sometimes seduced me into pitying all those who in the absence of sunlight huddle round a portable heater. And now that my sky is clouded over, I could use one myself, but I don't know how to deal with them. My interest, however, is great. What I can't handle and therefore don't know arouses my curiosity. Only too much! You were speaking warmly just now – use your momentum, tell the layman and philistine about your affairs.' I glanced at my watch and said, 'You speak in the plural, but I'm afraid the time is too short for more than one.' 'Then you'll just have to limit yourself. The agony of choice I can't spare you.' 'Good,' I said, 'is it all right with you if I stay with the bundle of nerves I've mentioned several times already?' 'That's up to you. The main thing is that I learn something from it.' 'I don't know what this case can teach you.' 'I just told you: how someone deals with a portable heater.'

'All right, then,' I said, 'I'll start at the beginning. It certainly isn't as interesting as your story about the dogs, but still appealing enough. The first phase is unquestionably the most appealing thing a relationship has to offer. There is nothing more exciting, more arousing, than gradually feeling your way into a relationship with a new woman! With looks, with words, and finally, if it crackles, with the play of hands and all that follows. I have an addict's craving for this crackle, but it seldom outlasts the early phase, and gradually gives way to a scrunch. Yes, yes, I know – you have another picture of it thanks to your experience. I have your sketch of the ladder still in my head. So then: I live in the outskirts of Bern, very close to a shopping centre that has a small park with a children's playground in it. There are also benches there and a splashing fountain. And one evening, after I had done some shopping, I saw a man standing at the fountain who was grinning idiotically and waving something back and forth in the water. I sat on a bench and watched him in amazement. He kept grinning and waving his object in the water. A woman came over, sat on the other end of the bench, and likewise watched. The man noticed our interest and seemed to enjoy it. Finally he took the thing out of the water and held it for a while under the stream from the pipe. I saw now that it was a set of dentures. The man fixed us with his gaze, opened his mouth wide, set the dentures in, and walked off grinning all the while. We looked at each other, the woman and I; she smiled, I laughed. She had a pretty, even beautiful face, and her almost black hair, which she wore cut short, offset its paleness. She wasn't my type, really – I go more for blondes and sporty women that I can play tennis with. Nevertheless I started talking to her, because I really don't have a choice. She said little, but her body language certainly didn't betray aloofness. I made a few casual generalisations about the rare form of exhibitionism we had just been allowed to witness. She seemed to find me very funny and thawed out to such an extent that I ventured to be bold and direct and asked if she would have an aperitif with me to celebrate April 1st. She asked if that was an April Fool's joke. 'No, utter seriousness,' I said. She smiled, looked at her watch, and hesitated. Then she said, as if to herself, 'Why not, actually?' And these three words she repeated again when I asked, after the Campari, if we could see each other again. My next question, however – whether I could carry her off to a nice restaurant – she answered with a no and set our rendezvous for the children's playground, at the same time the following week. With complete self-assurance she assumed the role I like to play in such cases, that of the master of the where and when. That she did so irritated me somewhat, but more than that it charmed me, for during the days of waiting I pictured the moment when the mistress of the situation would start to go weak at the knees. Incidentally, over our aperitifs I had learned as good as nothing about her, not even her first name, which made her all the more appealing to me. And there was a third attraction: I prefer more mature women, and she was that. She was somewhere close to forty, I estimated, an age at which women, in my experience, become maximally ripe for enjoyment.'

'Just a moment,' said Loos, 'I have to make a note of that expression, although...' He took his notebook out, but wrote nothing and stuck it away again. He pointed to his left forearm and said, 'The allergy.' And in fact I saw a few red bumps and asked him if he found the expression offensive. 'Applied to apricots or cheese, absolutely not,' he said, 'but just go on, I didn't mean to interrupt you.' 'Nor I to allergise you. In any case, she was wonderfully ripe, and my thoughts were orbiting daily round her and her appearance, which is usually taken as a symptom of being in love. But I was probably as little in love with her as the hound that follows the scent of the deer to the exclusion of any other thought. And yet I noticed, as I neared the playground for our appointed rendezvous, that my heart was knocking in my chest, something that had long stopped happening to me. She was already sitting on the bench, smoking, and was looking at the swing near the

fountain with such spellbound absorption that she didn't notice me
till I sat down beside her. Her greeting was disappointingly cursory,
and when I asked her how she was, she put her finger to her lips and
signalled with her head toward the swing. A little girl was sitting on
it, and beside her, leaning against the post, stood her presumed father
buried in a tabloid and giving the swing a push from time to time. It
wasn't clear to me why this should be so remarkable that I had to keep
still. "Yes, it's sweet," I said finally. "No, doctor, it's depressing," she said.
To my astonished question, how she knew that I had a doctor's title,
she said only that there were phonebooks. She had therefore occupied
herself with me; that was a good sign and every bit as encouraging as
her lips. They had not been made up at our first chance meeting, but
now they stood out dark red.

'We drank Campari again. She seemed relaxed. To my question
about the circumstances of her personal life she said, without being
brusque, that she suggested we give up investigating each other's lives.
Her profession was the only thing she divulged: she was a caretaker in
a home for the handicapped. I couldn't help asking, despite her suggestion, whether she was married. She gave a slight nod. It suited me
that she *was* married, I felt freer that way: it was more challenging and
aroused my lust for conquest, so to speak. In addition, I clearly sensed –
I'm not exactly without instincts – that something about me appealed
to her. But after an hour – I was just about to ask her if I really had to
go alone now to get something to eat – she stood up and said, "In a
week?" "Couldn't it be sooner?" I asked. "In a week. I'm sure you know
where." She had me so much on tenterhooks, she had brought me to
such a pass, and I doubt she was at all conscious of tactics, that I was
much more intensely preoccupied with her the following week than I
had been in the previous. Maybe I really was in love at this point, but I
remembered Tasso's adage: "Being in love is happiness of the soul, with
the sensual appetite in a wholly decent accompaniment." Mine wasn't
decent; it was, I admit it, tyrannically dominant.

'Now I rigorously abbreviate. The third time everything was

different. She seemed rejuvenated, buoyant, as high-spirited as a girl. She wasn't sitting on the bench when I arrived, she was sitting on the swing and greeted me with a beaming expression. Then she drank water from the pipe, saw a bird's feather in the fountain, and fished it out. "Come," she said and walked over to the sand heap in the corner of the playground. Now she's going to build a sand castle, I thought. But she did something else, she used the quill to write the name VALERIE in the sand. "Thank you," I said. "You've made it exciting. For two whole weeks you've condemned me to dreaming about a woman I knew only as Mrs Bendel." "You could have just asked me," she said. "I asked you twice," I replied, "you apparently didn't hear it." "Let's not fight about it," she said, "because I'm hungry." "OK," I said, very pleased, "I'll go get a taxi." "Don't say OK, please, I hate that imported expression." "All right," I said. "Are you going to find fault with my nose next?" "Show!" she said. I dutifully lowered my head. She inspected it and said, "It's OK."

'Over dinner – we ate Chateaubriand and drank a wonderfully spicy Chambertin – I asked her why she was suddenly so changed, so light and cheerful. "To suit you better, and because yesterday and tomorrow don't weigh me down for once." "I'm glad," I said. "It's the same with me, and not for once, but most of the time." "I know, I know. I saw that from the first. A loose bird doesn't have to 'out itself '." "Good," I said, "then it will hardly surprise you if I ask you to come to my place for a little while." She hesitated and considered it, then said, "Why not, actually?" She stayed until two in the morning, and I can tell you, it was like a dream.'

'Oh God,' Loos said, 'how free you all are!' 'You are too,' I said, 'and as a mature protector type, you could have as many women as you do fingers, any time you wanted, and young ones too.' 'Yes,' said Loos. '"Free I am, and nothing seems more worthless to me." The gloomy words aren't mine, but they describe me perfectly. But this is by the by. How was she in bed then?' I looked at Loos uncertainly. The question didn't fit him, which is why I thought he asked it to make fun of me and my heroics, but perhaps also to test my levels of taste and discretion. With a certain ill humour I said to him that I didn't have the impression that the answer would interest him. 'You've put exciting fare on my table,' he said, 'but you want to deny me the dessert?' I laughed and said, 'All right then, from man to man, she was fantastic, she was – how shall I say? – passionate in a strangely reserved way, cried out with her mouth gagged, so to speak. Is that good enough?' 'Completely,' said Loos. He drank, choked, coughed, and then asked with a throaty voice, 'How did the affair go afterwards? How did it end, and why?' 'I'd like to take a rest now,' I said, 'and listen to you again.' 'Just as you like, but you have to help me: where did I stop?' 'Hard to say. The last thing you told me was how you and your wife got together with the help of two dogs. But that was more of an excursus, you had actually stopped before that in the history of your wife's illness.'

'Right, yes, with the astrocytoma. When I told her that *astro* comes from the Greek *astron* and means *star*, while *cytus*, Latin for *cell*, comes from the Greek *kytos* which is like *hollow* or *cavity*, she smiled dreamily and spoke no more about a swelling or a tumour but about a star in her skull cavity or simply about her star. "My star," she said from then on, and not "my tumour". And since she at times was a little extravagant, she would also say that a star could never be her enemy. And it even seemed actually – I've hinted at this – as though she looked death in the eye not stiff with fright, but somehow almost tenderly. For a while I was afraid that she might refuse to have an operation, which she fortunately did not do, severely tormented as she was by her symptoms. They didn't know, by the way, whether the tumour was benign or malignant – that only the operation could show, and its outcome was described to us as very promising, because of the favourable position of the tumour, and in the best case would not entail follow-up treatment with radiation or chemotherapy. In the not very long waiting period I took care of all household matters and read all Bettina's wishes in her eyes. The latter was nothing new, but the former certainly was. I bought myself a cookbook without her knowing it, a vegetarian one of course, and studied it in school while the pupils where doing their work. I made a list of the ingredients, bought the necessaries, and surprised my wife almost every evening with some small gourmet menu. Of course, her appetite was slight, and mine as well, since my constant anxiety about the worst, the truly unimaginable, seemed to narrow both my windpipe and my oesophagus. It was not a great time, and yet it was. We still had ourselves, we were one. I was relieved and happy when I saw Bettina reading a book with the title *A Hundred Steps to Happiness*. It showed me that she hadn't closed herself off, that she was still oriented to life. At the same time it made me wonder why she consulted a book like that for advice. Apart from her present suffering she had always been happy. Even with me. Perhaps not always, of course – happiness isn't a steady state, is it? Otherwise we wouldn't feel it. It's lack of happiness that seems to be the steady state. But the point is, she was reading that kind of book, and yet could say to me out of the blue that she wanted no grave decorations, especially no wreaths or so-called floral tributes with pine cones and the like. We seldom had differences of taste, and certainly not in this matter, and yet it took away my power of speech when she said that. Now, for the first time, we switched roles. I was the pessimist practising confidence and adopting positive thinking, while her vision grew ever darker, and though she never complained or surrendered to anxiety, she was utterly fatalistic. She would probably die while under the knife, she said, though she had been informed that such deaths were rare even with this ticklish kind of surgery. The fatality rate for this type of operation was not even as high as two per cent, yet my wife insisted that she was in this group. When I asked what prompted this belief, she said, "The star wants to remain in me, it will defend itself." That's all she said; more I could not get out of her.

After that everything went well, very well even. They spoke of an ideal case, because, first, the team of surgeons were able to remove the whole tumour from the brain and, second, the tissue sample showed that though the tumour wasn't altogether benign, it was, as the doctors put it, *still* benign. And there were no complications after surgery, so that we could say without exaggeration that Bettina was cured. I visited her as often as I could and held her hand. She hardly spoke, she was infinitely languid or lacklustre, and I attributed this to the fact that she was so often in tears and that she didn't have the energy to express joy and relief whether with words or with her shrouded glances. "You've been given back to me as a gift," I told her and was troubled that her hand remained practically lifeless in mine.

'When I returned home after hospital visits her emptiness passed into me. I sat around without purpose, and because I was incapable of busying myself with anything meaningful, I watched television for hours, receptive to the stupidest drivel, and was afraid of going to bed. My sleep was superficial, little more than a half-sleep from which I was sometimes jolted awake by words of love I was murmuring in my sleep or by the mere name Bettina, which I'll say in passing I always loved because it sounds so downy soft. Twelve years is a long time, and when you're suddenly lying alone in bed, it's as if you've lost your own self, as if you can't yourself breathe because the other's breathing isn't there. And yet I don't think we ever became props for each other, because props you take for granted and use them unconsciously. Dull habit, which I admit often creeps into marriages and can lead to a state where you hardly look at each other, had – who knows why? – spared us. Whether you believe it or not.'

'Why shouldn't I believe it?' 'Well, I know what you think of marriage,' Loos said. 'You've expressed yourself on that clearly enough, telling me about your clients' standard sigh: "The thing has gone dead." And you will also have heard the phrase outside your practice, in the context of your escapades, from those same married women who fall for your charm because they're in a dead relationship – from this Amelie you just told me about, for instance. So you're continually confirmed in your belief about the perversity of marriage.' 'In the first place, her name wasn't Amelie, but Valerie, and in the second, she never disparaged the relationship she was in, never used it as justification for her behaviour, at least not with me. She never spoke of it at all, as often as I tried to entice something out of her. She said virtually nothing about her husband, and much less anything negative, which made me a little jealous – as did the thought that she could keep sleeping with her musician as if nothing had happened. Because I did learn that he was a musician, or more exactly, a cello teacher. Also that his name was Felix. So you see that you chose a bad example, though I admit that you're partly right. I have in fact met women who start complaining about their marriages and their deficient husbands after the first kiss. But that's a warning signal for me. When a marriage is failing and then another man comes into the picture, the woman starts gathering courage to make the leap, in the belief that he will be the safety net to catch her if she falls. That's not my role. I refuse to be thought of as a serious alternative. What I want is a playful scuffle, and I don't hide that from any woman, and if she nevertheless begins to cling, then I break it off. And incidentally, in my experience, it isn't just unsatisfied, unfulfilled women who can be led to temptation. I have observed a different and not at all uncommon phenomenon both as an outsider as well as sometimes within my own experience, a phenomenon I welcome. Women who are in good hands and feel very secure in them often seem to need something different. They love their husband as a calming influence and feel the marriage as a refuge, an emotional mainland that they want to keep standing on. And yet something is missing. And yet the open sea, restless and unpredictable, exerts a strong power of attraction over them. What speaks against a stimulating swim with a hint of danger in it? Actually nothing, as long as the mainland stays within sight. Do you see what I mean? The hot water bottle is reliable and radiates a comfortable warmth; more romantic and crackling, by contrast, is a fire.'

'Yes, I understand,' Loos said. 'Husbands are the hot water bottles and you're the fiery devil. What you say may not be entirely wrong, only you act as if the plunge into the tempestuous sea were typically a woman's dream. There are also married men who don't want to do without their cozy little wife and ironer-of-shirts, but still feel free to dance at a second, more glamorous wedding, so to speak – to have their cake and eat it too. I myself never had the urge to be elsewhere involved, and for the simple reason that my wife was so rich and multifaceted that I felt not the slightest lack: she gave me everything and was everything to me. But never mind that – what I still want to ask is which of the two infidelity groups you put Valerie in? Did she come from a failing marriage or an intact one?' 'I was never able to find that out,' I said. 'As I said, she didn't want to talk about it. It was altogether as if she came out of nowhere, as if she had no previous life, no history, and I'm convinced that that for her was the most exciting thing about our affair. I noticed how she enjoyed being a blank page to write on and surprising me, and probably herself, with everything she said, desired or did. I believe that she became new to herself by feeling how excitingly new she was for me. I too enjoyed it of course – having a lover who lightened me of all ballast and had no need to define our relationship or alarm me with hinting remarks about the future. One day, about five weeks after we met, I did get alarmed. We had gone dancing – we both loved the tango – and I asked her on the way back to my place why she suddenly had more time for me, how she explained her frequent goings-out at home. "Let that be my concern," she said bluntly, but for once I didn't let up until I found out from her that she was living with her sister. And then I got alarmed. What else could I conclude but that she had left her husband for my sake? We had mutually agreed, without ever saying so, to keep the relationship delightfully uncomplicated. I had been of the opinion that Valerie too regarded it as a romance, enjoyed it as such, and saw in it no reason to shake the marriage. I expostulated with her and called her move a bad decision. I asked her why she would endanger an established thing and leave the husband she had never spoken ill of in the lurch. It all sounded as if I had the closest brotherly sympathy for him. But I imagine she saw through me and recognised the reason for my chagrin. In any case she said, as if to comfort me, that it was a matter of a temporary separation, a pause for breath. I had already asked her several times whether her husband knew anything about us and never received an answer. Now I could assume he had the picture. She countered with the question of why this was of such burning interest to me. I didn't know; I think it just irritated me that she marked off zones that were inaccessible to me. That evening I made love to her with an almost angry vehemence, without any foreplay.'

Loos yawned and looked at the clock. 'I see you're bored,' I said to him, 'and I can even understand it. You're thinking of your wife, of the anniversary of her death tomorrow maybe, and here I torture you with stories of my affairs and rehash old events.' 'A person has to be allowed to yawn,' said Loos. 'That has to do with lack of oxygen, not disinterest. What seems inconsequential to you strikes me, an amateur standing on the sidelines, as very interesting. Are you walking back to Agra?' 'It would be more reasonable. Why do you ask?' 'First because the staff here have long been waiting for us to go, and second because I'd like to go with you. You still owe me, after all, the continuation as well as the conclusion of the story.' 'Good, I'd be glad to. I assume you know that you still owe me something too.' 'One thing at a time,' Loos said.

I got my umbrella, which I had left on the terrace. Loos, tottering a bit, asked me to hold him up – he needed a third leg. We walked through the village. When we passed the butcher's shop Loos stopped and said, 'Flesh is capricious.' What did he mean by that, I asked, but he gave no reply. But after a while he gave me the cue to go ahead with my story. 'Let me sum up,' he said. 'The moment Amelie got herself more freedom by moving out of her home you felt yours threatened, is that right?' 'Her name was of course Valerie, but otherwise you describe the situation correctly. As much as it delighted me to be with her far more often than before, I was equally worried that her heavier tread might suddenly weigh down the wonderful lightness of what we had had up to now. I'm not made for a close bond, in this department *I* am the amateur.' 'Are you really sure that she wanted what filled you with dread? Were there any other signs of that than her change of residence?

Did she, for example, speak of love?' 'No, not that,' I said. 'She avoided doing and saying anything that she seemed to think might oppress me. But it was precisely that that showed me how much it mattered to her not to lose me. Sometimes she would withdraw from me, sometimes she wouldn't show up at a rendezvous – both without giving a reason and both, I'm convinced of this, to accommodate me, to demonstrate that she was independent and uncommitted. And there were still other signs. I've already said that in the beginning Valerie divulged very little about herself and kept her past in the past. That didn't bother me, just the opposite: we lived only in the present like all intoxicated people. Only it was strange that even later, when we saw each other almost daily, she did not become much more talkative. Perhaps, as I suspected, it was because I had let her know early in our relationship how exciting I found it to have a veiled woman for a lover. In other words, it could be that she wanted to remain exciting to me by continuing to conceal herself and holding her silence. And finally there was a third indication. After the great delirium, on my part at least, had faded, Valerie changed somewhat. She got more serious. The unselfconscious buoyancy that I so liked about her suddenly became more forced. She didn't like to joke around any more, and when she did, it might happen that she abruptly flung her arms around my neck and shed a few tears. In short, all of this made me worry: it all seemed to show how different our two desires had suddenly become. And I started hearing, though only in the distance as yet, that old and hackneyed song: the man has only an affair in mind, the woman wants a relationship. If I wanted to be malicious I could sing the rest of the ditty: once her desire for a lasting relationship, for a reliable partner who will provide her with security, is fulfilled, she will sooner or later start to feel that something is missing, something spicy, tingly, piquant. The woman always wants both, and the man who can be both – a beloved companion and a coveted faun – has yet to be born.'

'You repeat yourself,' said Loos, 'and a repeated half-truth doesn't make a whole one. Tell me instead how you warded off the bane of a solid bond. How long altogether did the loose one last?' 'Barely a quarter of a year,' I said, 'and by half that time – once I thought I saw that Valerie was too attached to me – I began making myself scarcer. I invoked professional demands. We saw each other less often, but actually, when we did see each other, it was just as sweet as it was before, sensually above all. That probably had to do with the fact that her body was the only thing I could hold on to – her inner life she kept partly hidden. Her body could be grasped, as almost nothing else about her could, and her tendency to make herself mysterious, and thus interesting, gradually started to drive me up the wall.'

'Hold on,' said Loos, 'I've got to go.' 'So do I actually,' I said. We stood, as we had the night before, off the edge of the road. 'There are flowers,' Loos said, 'that don't open unless the sun shines on them. They feel the sunlight as a sort of acceptance, something protective, and its lack makes them withdraw into themselves, hide themselves, as it were.' 'Very poetic,' I said, 'very metaphorical. Can you put it more directly?' 'Yes,' said Loos, 'I can do that: I feel sorry for this woman.' 'First of all, I'm not a monster,' I said, 'and second, she knew exactly what, and what kind of person, she was getting involved in and with. If she was looking for a safe haven, then she would have steered clear of me.'

Loos was quiet. He needed more time than I did, so I went a few steps ahead. When he started coming after me – I heard only the metallic tap of the umbrella tip on the pavement – I was hit by a wave of anxiety for several seconds. I felt pursued, for no reason I could think of, as if I were about to be hit with a blow from behind. Loos caught up with me. 'I wasn't going to attack you,' he said, as if he knew about my bout of panic. But he went on without alluding to it: 'You've made me feel I know Valerie, the way you did with Tasso; you've aroused my sympathy for her, that's all.' 'I'm relieved, then' I said, 'because I felt your sympathy as a reproach, and I have nothing to reproach myself with really, unless it's my cowardice. I hesitated too long about pouring her a clear glass of wine, so to speak, about telling her that a separation would be better for both of us. And yet even my hesitation had its reasons. I was trying to be considerate of her nervous condition, which was never optimal and during the third month of our relationship deteriorated alarmingly. Crying fits, sleeplessness, convulsions: it was virtual torture. Naturally I asked her whether she knew what was causing the trouble, and she spoke of problems in the handicapped-home, the gruelling work, conflicts among the staff, etc. I advised her to do something about it, see a psychiatrist. She did that after a protracted resistance. The doctor recommended a stay at the Cademario Sanatorium, and she travelled down there in June. I called her up from time to time; she seemed rather cool and never said that she missed me, which was every bit as much of a relief to me as her telling me she was feeling better every day. I assumed then, actually, that the distance from me and the relaxing escape from daily life had given her the chance to take stock of herself, to realise, in other words, that the time had come to separate. I thought it would be possible for us to do that amicably, and during the third and last week of her stay, I pulled myself together for it. To wait until Valerie got back would be lazy, and not altogether advisable, since we had to worry about sinking back into the old habits and losing our nerve for the final stroke. I called her the day before I visited. She was looking forward to seeing me – more than I liked.

'So I drove down and arrived at Cademario in the afternoon, just before four. She was sitting on the terrace of the sanatorium restaurant drinking coffee with an extremely attractive woman in a white uniform. Valerie looked relaxed, greeted me affectionately, and introduced me to Eva, a respiratory therapist. They seemed to have become good friends. Eva wanted to go, but Valerie wouldn't let her. She said jokingly that I found it hard to be alone, and that she should keep me company, now that we were introduced, while she went and got herself ready for the evening. I was on top form talking to Eva, effortlessly casual. She was exactly my type: sporty, lively, sexy. I can say that I have a certain amount of experience in this sort of thing, but the fact that there was such a quick spark between us surprised even me a little. Her catlike eyes flashed unambiguously – I'm not blind! And since I'm also not a fool, I told her it was a pity that her coffee break would soon be over. She said she couldn't spare me that pity, but on the other hand she was free the whole next day, if I were still in the area. I said that I had planned to go home tomorrow, but was ready in an emergency to alter that plan. "Here – for the emergency," she said, giving me her card, and left the terrace with an elastic step. You're probably surprised how unembarrassed she was about coming on to me, despite knowing for certain that I was connected with Valerie. I myself was not much surprised, because in these things women are without scruples – I've seen it many times. As soon as a man arouses their erotic interest, they treat the woman he's with like a negligible quantity, if not a rival. The female nature knows nothing of sisterly regard.'

Loos stopped, breathing heavily in a slightly stooped posture with both hands propped on the umbrella. It was so deathly still I could hear him clacking his teeth together a few times. 'Are you all right?' I asked. 'Yes, yes, of course' he said. 'It's just that the strain of admiring you tires me out. You acted with brotherly regard for Valerie's husband when you went after his wife. You had a hundred scruples about flirting with Eva while Valerie was making herself beautiful for you. The male nature is simply nobler. Let's go, it's almost midnight.'

'Well, yes,' I said, 'I admit my flirting with Eva wasn't completely above board. Nothing came of it, by the way, except a steamy little roll in the hay the next afternoon, she clearly didn't want anything more. I called several times afterwards suggesting we get together, but she always put me off, and the thing ended there.' 'And what happened with Valerie afterwards?' Loos asked. 'How did the evening with her go?' 'Subdued,' I said, 'although she was as cheerful as she was in our first days together and seemed completely recovered. The only thing was, she had had an injury. I only noticed it when she came back out to the terrace. Her ring finger was in a splint. She had stupidly stumbled over a branch on a walk in the woods, as she put it, and broken her finger in her first week there. When I asked why she had never said so much as a word about the accident in our phone conversations, she simply said that she hadn't wanted to seem self-pitying. We chatted on the drive to Agra, with a stop in Agno, where I filled the tank and Valerie got cigarettes and a ladies' magazine. It smelled a little musty in the house, and the air was stifling, so I opened the shutters and the windows. Valerie hugged me. I said I had to make a quick business call, poured her a Cynar, and went into the garden, where I called my secretary to ask her to reschedule the two appointments I had for the next day. When I came back, Valerie was sitting on the sofa thumbing through her magazine. She asked if I knew what the longest lifespan of a housefly was. "No," I said. "Only six and a half days," she said. I said that was a respectable age compared with a mayfly. She stood up and gave me another hug. "You seem a little shy," she said. "What's up?" "Nothing," I said, "I'm just a little stressed." She asked if she should massage me. I said I was hungry, and we drove down to the Bellevue. She ate with appetite, but I had a knot in my throat. She was brightly chirping to me about her stay in the sanatorium and how she had become friends with Eva – did I like her? I said I thought she was really nice, and then I suddenly felt suspicious.'

'I know what you mean,' said Loos. 'I had a moment's suspicion too, but I don't think that Valerie, as I know her from your description, would be capable even of thinking of guile. She would never have asked Eva to play the decoy to test your fidelity.' 'Your x-ray vision frightens me,' I said. 'That was in fact what I suspected, but I too rejected it immediately. To cut a long story short, however: I had actually planned to direct the conversation to our relationship and to tell Valerie as considerately as possible that it wasn't working for me anymore, that I had the impression I was the wrong one for her and wasn't giving her what she expected. But I couldn't bring it off. She was so sweet and cheerful, I just couldn't do it. I bided my time and deliberately kept my talk to a minimum in the hope that she'd ask a second time what was up with me. But she didn't. I brought her back to Cademario around ten. She was humming in the car. I went with her to her room – she wanted me to see it. There was a table with a bottle of red and two glasses on it, and next to it a television set that she had covered with a small cloth. She opened the bottle – something I would usually have done – and filled the glasses full. She sat on the bed, I in the armchair. "To the two of us!" she said, took a sip, put the glass down on the night table, and lay down. "Valerie…" I started. "Thomas," she said shyly, "come over here for just a minute, I mean in your clothes, just to sit." I couldn't move, and she sat up. "I'll cope with it," she said. "With what?" I asked. "What you want to tell me," she said. Then she listened, calmly, except that sometimes her chin trembled. She nodded when I was through, as if she agreed. She asked no questions. In a soft, hardly audible voice she said, "I feel pathetic." After a while, she stood up and opened the door. "Flee!" she said.

'And that's it. We never saw or heard anything from each other again. I say that without regret and assume that Valerie quickly got over the break-up, otherwise she wouldn't have kept so consistently out of sight, she would have raised hell for some time to come.' 'Maybe she returned to her traditional anchorage?' said Loos. 'Could be,' I said. 'They certainly say there are men who take their wives into their arms and console them when they come crying back home after a bitter disappointment.' 'Did she have any children at all?' Loos asked. 'No,' I said, 'she never wanted any. The world was full enough, she once said, and any new football fan was one too many. She meant that as a joke, of course, because she knew that I was one. The real reasons she kept to herself, as usual. Why do you ask?' 'To round out my picture,' Loos replied. 'A waste of time and effort,' I said. 'If *I* can't even form a picture of this ultimately unknown woman, how are you going to round out yours?' 'The blank spaces also belong to the text,' Loos said, 'and if it's the way you think it is, then I'll simply round out a phantom picture.'

It was past twelve when we got to the house. I wasn't tired and suggested we still have a nightcap. Loos didn't resist. I made a fire in the fireplace while he stood pensively beside me. He pointed to the sofa and asked whether this was Tasso's deathbed. It stood in the same place, I said, but we had had to take it out and burn it. I moved the two arm-chairs up to the fireplace, filled the cognac glasses, and asked what we should toast to. 'To the witching hour, when ghosts appear,' he said. I asked whether he believed in ghosts. He stared into the flames and said nothing. I looked at his face, which seemed to keep changing in the flickering firelight. He suddenly said that the open fire reminded him of a ballad called 'Feet in the Fire,' Conrad Meyer, did I know it? I said we had read it once in school – I couldn't remember what it was about, except for one detail that must have impressed me. Wasn't there a man in it who for some reason turned grey overnight? That was no detail, Loos said, continuing to stare into the fire. I asked him to tell me the ballad's story. He shook his head. If he wanted to be alone, I told him, I would retire. I well knew, I said, what he wanted to think about. He could sleep here overnight, either in the chair or on the sofa. He said he still owed me the final account of what had happened a year ago, at least the part of it that had a hold on his soul. The time before his wife was released from the hospital had been empty, as if it had come to a stop. That time was still passing he recognised only by the slowly filling garbage pail. His happiness was great when Bettina came home, and yet also clouded again by the prospect of having to do without her, since a convalescent separation was unavoidable. Now that there was, thank God, no need for post-operative treatment with radiation etc., she could pick any place she liked for her stay. She studied various prospectuses, including one for the Cademario Sanatorium and Well-ness Hotel. And because she remembered that on the occasion of their Hesse weekend in Montagnola the two of them had snuggled up to each other in their Bellevue hotel room looking out across the valley and the gleaming lake to the chain of hills and the village with its massive sanatorium nestled high up on one of them – because Bettina remembered this, she immediately made her decision. He, however, had expressed his reservations about it: he would rather have had her in closer proximity, so that he could visit her as often as possible. She thereupon said that the best and simplest thing would be that they go on vacation together. He lost no time in going to the school rector and asking for a week off, which was granted him – naturally on condition that he make the time up. Bettina was delighted, just as, in general, her mood had become more glad-hearted day by day, despite occasional bouts of listlessness. The words *glad-hearted* had an archaic ring, of course, Loos said, but they fitted. So they booked a room for two with a view to the south and a balcony, and at the start of the second week of June they drove down together in the car to have more freedom. He didn't need to describe the sanatorium hotel or the spectacular view it afforded, since I had seen both. They were standing on the balcony with their arms propped on the railings, looking into the distance and also, with slight vertigo, down into the depths of the valley. For the suicidal, Bettina had said, the railing – which didn't reach even to her navel – presented a dangerously low barrier. He had countered that one wouldn't exactly expect potential suicides to come to a wellness hotel. She conceded the point and gave him her hand. They stood on the balcony and felt like newlyweds. And their first night was really the epitome of a wedding night, at least partially. At this point he had to mention, as embarrassed as he was to do so, a kind of illness that still oppressed him today. He suffered from bruxism.

Loos took a sip of cognac. I said, 'Never heard of it. A male condition?' He shook his head. Bruxism was the medical term for nocturnal grinding of the teeth, or more exactly, for the grinding of the teeth in sleep. He himself hardly noticed it. Sometimes it didn't occur, though other times it was very bad, in which case it might happen that the grinding woke him up and that the next morning he had pain in his jaws – complaints of the masticatory musculature – and sometimes even earaches. And precisely then, at Cademario, of all times, fate had been malicious enough to prescribe him a bout of pronounced grinding that outdid anything he had known before. The grinding itself would probably have been bearable – it was not a loud noise – but with him unfortunately it very often alternated with snoring, and the two together were of course too much for a fellow human being to endure. Bettina had hardly shut an eye that first night and was a wreck the next day. They discussed the problem, and it was clear to him that his grinding and snoring were completely ruining Bettina's sleep and her recuperation along with it, so he suggested they sleep in separate rooms. Bettina protested at first, but then reluctantly agreed. He tried to get a room at the sanatorium, a single of course, but, annoyingly, they were all taken. To rent a second double was hardly in question in view of the price.

They were standing on the balcony discussing this, when his wife had lifted her arm, pointed to the elevation of the Collina d'Oro on the other side of the valley, and said, 'Why not go to our Bellevue!' That had made a lot of sense to him, despite the more than four kilometres straight across that would separate them while they slept. And they did not regret adopting this solution, on the contrary: it became something special to take leave of each other every night and find each other – and themselves – again the next morning, it intensified their feeling of attachment. It was like a return of their love's spring, except that their married life had never really entered an autumnal period. They hadn't made any connections with other guests: they only needed each other and went walking for hours in the woods of chestnut and birch, although with rests. Once Bettina said that she was a little anxious about returning to the real world, to which he countered that birch woods too belonged to the real world. Yes, she said, only no one heard the tumult of war in them. She was alluding to the Kosovan war, which had deeply upset her. 'Do you know?' she went on, 'I feel the atrocities there like blows to my own head; they daze me and rob me of clear-sightedness.' He had replied that it affected many people the same way, and that it was something creditable, because numbness only strengthened the perpetrators. Then one could also say, Bettina observed, that bewilderment was both a decent and an indecent response to a devastating madness. So it seemed, he had said to her, and she hugged him passionately and squeezed herself against

him, as if to say that there was still also something utterly uncomplicated on earth.

He had taken Bettina out twice and drunk a Bianco di Merlot with
her on the Bellevue terrace. She had said she thought he might be able
to see across to her balcony at the resort from here, or better from his
room, at least if he had a telescope and she was waving her white bathrobe. Feeling a little foolish he bought one of the smaller telescopes
in Lugano. On the morning of the fourth day, at 9 am sharp, with
the atmosphere clear and the resort in full sunlight, they performed
the test with smashing success. He could see it clearly, Bettina's white
bathrobe, clearly, though it hardly looked bigger than a handkerchief.
Then he drove over as he did every morning to have breakfast with
Bettina. She hadn't yet got dressed, and he marvelled once again at
how enchanting she looked in her white bathrobe and the orange kerchief wrapped like a turban around her head. She reacted with childlike pleasure when he told her that he had been able to see her waving
– he would never forget the delight in her eyes. No valley, he had then
thought, no valley was wide enough to separate him from Bettina.
While she was dressing they arranged to repeat the waving game the
next day, again at nine, after her swim – she swam every day from 8:30
in the indoor pool. Then they had breakfast, and he couldn't recall
what they did for the rest of the day.

'You see, Mr Clarin,' said Loos and turned his gaze from the fire to
me for the first time, 'you see now how right I was about the licking
flames at Pentecost.' 'Thomas,' I said, 'why the "Mister"?' He didn't
hear me, he was looking steadily into the flames again. Minutes went
by. 'Fresh raspberries,' he said suddenly. 'I remember those. They
gave them to us that evening for dessert.' 'I know,' I said. 'Your wife
ordered them as an appetiser because she was afraid they might be
eaten up by the others before she was through with the main course.'
'He knows shit,' Loos murmured. Although it seemed clear to me that
he was thinking out loud, probably without realising it, I was pretty
bewildered and couldn't explain his crassness any more than I could

his return to the "Mister". Minutes went by again. He was crumpling visibly. I stood up and brought him a glass of water. 'You should have brought handcuffs,' he said, before drinking the water. 'For me or for you?' I asked. 'For me, naturally,' he said. I asked what crime he'd committed. He didn't answer. He straightened his body. Then he said, 'I'm sorry, I got a little confused. I'm feeling better now. I think I can finish. Don't put another log on, I'll make it short.'

'We sat on her balcony for a long time after the dinner that evening. I don't remember what we talked about. I only remember that my wife cried when we said goodbye. I said I'd be back again very soon. But she couldn't be consoled because, she said, she was weeping for happiness. The next morning, a Friday, the eleventh of June, I stood ahead of time at my window. It was another clear day, and the telescope on the tripod was in sharp focus. From sheer worry that I'd miss Bettina's appearance I started looking at ten before nine. By nine I was already impatient when she didn't appear at the stroke of the bell. She was usually very punctual. It got to be five past, ten past – no white bathrobe waving. Although I naturally told myself that she might have overslept or been detained at the pool by a conversation, or even that she had forgotten our arrangement, I became more and more nervous. I called her room number, and she didn't answer. I waited till 9:30, tried to call her again, unsuccessfully, and then drove over – half-irritated, half-concerned – and up the hill to the sanatorium. The door to her room was locked. I knocked for a while – nothing. Then I took a quick look in the pool area and, just to be sure, in the exercise room. She wasn't on the terrace either, or in the dining room, so I started looking for her in the park, by the outdoor pool, even in the greenhouse for cactuses. Nothing. I hurried back to the building, climbed the stairs, and knocked on Bettina's door again. Then I went to the reception desk and, still panting, asked after my wife. The two women there looked at each other and both said, 'There you are, at last!' One of them asked me in a low voice to come into her office behind the desk. She said that they hadn't been able to give me the news, nobody knew where I was staying. It was her unpleasant task to tell me that my wife had had an accident in the pool, at 8:30. She had slipped on the edge and hurt herself falling – apparently a blow to the back of the head, otherwise she would not have lost consciousness. It might not be dangerous. They immediately took her to the Ospedale Civico in Lugano – did I wanted to call there right now? "I'll drive there," I said and listened without comprehension to the directions she was giving me. After a number of wrong turns, I arrived at the hospital around noon and was brought to the intensive care unit. Bettina had waited for me, even if unconsciously. She didn't close her eyes until I got there and her hand lay in mine. As her hand went cold, so did I. That's the only thing I can remember, all the rest of it is gone. All the decisions and arrangements I made mechanically. It took two weeks for the feeling of numbness to recede, and that only happened when I opened her wardrobe for the first time. The sight of her dresses, skirts, blouses, jackets, hanging dead yet expectant on the hangers, redeemed me – I felt the frozen block in me melt away in an instant. And shortly after, I found in the little storage space next to her room three new, unused, blue suitcases that I had never seen before. I couldn't explain either how they got there or why I was so moved to see them there.'

Loos stopped. I asked in a low voice what Bettina had died of. Her large kerchief, he said, though piled up into a kind of turban, was too little to soften the impact. She had presumably died of a brain hemorrhage, though that was not verified. He had refused an autopsy. It was far more important for him to protect his wife's body from the hands of strangers than to know the cause of her death.

'Thomas,' I said, 'I am deeply sorry to hear all this. I hope as a friend, if you'll allow me to call myself that, that you will eventually get over it.' 'I'm already halfway there,' Loos said and stood up. 'You are, incidentally, the first and only person who's heard my story. I say this only in passing. And now I'll be on my way.' 'Listen,' I said, 'I don't want to be a nuisance, but I'd like to see you again, just briefly. I'm getting the car in the morning.' Loos thought. 'I'm going to sleep late,' he said.

'Around eleven I'll be sitting on the terrace, as far as conditions allow.' 'I'll come,' I said. 'I'd be delighted.'

I accompanied him to the garden gate, where he stopped and stood indecisively. I said, 'So – till tomorrow. Have good dreams tonight.' He seemed not to hear me, or to notice my outstretched hand. The moon had set, and it was very quiet. I could hear only the light rustling of the bamboo hedge next to us and – it sounded somewhat eerie – the clacking of teeth. Was something wrong, I asked? Would he like to stay overnight after all? 'You've helped me, Mr Clarin. Thank you,' he said. 'In what way?' I asked. 'You've helped me very much, Thomas,' he said. 'I was glad to listen to you,' I said. 'You don't need to thank me for it. And if I rightly understand you, that it's relieved you to be able to talk – I think that's wonderful.' Loos took a step toward me and said in a strained voice close to my ear, 'Lay yourself to sleep with your false interpretation, and don't forget to bolt the door.'

Then he turned away without a word of goodbye and disappeared into the darkness.

III

ALTHOUGH I SAT for almost another hour in front of the cooling ashes, I could find no explanation for his strange departure. I could only assume that by bringing the tragic events back to life in his narration Loos had fallen into a state where his inner turmoil expressed itself in disoriented behaviour. If that was the case, then it seemed pointless to try to interpret his behaviour and find some meaning in his final words.

I went to bed. Loos kept circling through my mind. I would gladly have dismissed him as a lunatic so that I could calm down. I thought about the handcuffs. If somebody wants to be handcuffed, it means he has guilty feelings. If someone has guilty feelings, it means he's assumed guilt. It doesn't necessarily mean he's a murderer. It doesn't necessarily mean that he killed his wife by drowning her in the indoor pool. It doesn't necessarily mean that she had an accident there. She never slipped. Loos has concocted a version of her death that exonerates him. Here's the way it really happened: he drank too much and then lost control over the car on one of the hairpin bends on the road to Cademario, resulting in the death of his wife, for example. For another example: he's sitting in the room at the sanatorium while she stands out on the balcony. From the chair he sees how she bends over the railing, farther and farther, and he jumps up and cries 'Bettina!' – and she falls the moment he cries out. And ever since: guilty feelings and lunacy. Makes perfect sense. 'Don't forget to bolt the door!' In other words: 'Protect yourself from me, I'm a criminal!' 'Lay yourself to sleep with your false interpretation!' In other words: 'How can I feel relieved and free, when only I know the truth?' Just one thing remained unclear: why and for what purpose did Loos thank me? What can I have helped him with? I'll ask him again tomorrow. He completely confided in me, as the 'only one,' he said. He likes me. Why should he lie to me? What would he gain? A pool accident resulting in death: what's unbelievable about that? Bettina was brought to the hospital and died. No health resort in the world would broadcast such an incident. 'Checked out early,' they would say, if asked. I would like to finally get to sleep. Loos may or may not be mentally disturbed, but I would like to sleep. Or I could call Francisca, it's her profession. She once claimed that everyone, psychologically speaking, oversteps the clandestine boundary between sick and normal several times a day. Absurd. As if we all have one foot in the nuthouse. Good night!

Pentecost Sunday. After a miserable sleep, in which my dreams were confused and preposterous, I got up at nine. I felt better than on the previous day. I could have worked now and was irritated by the eleven o'clock appointment. It surprised me that I had let myself in for it just like that, without thinking for a second about my obligation or the project itself. That's how strong Loos's hold on me was. I felt I'd had a surfeit, a Loos-surfeit. I felt the way I often feel after one-night stands. Animated by wine and lust, I'd feel fulfilled and somehow remote from the world for a few hours, and then I'd wake up in the morning with the touch of a strange woman's foot and shrink back with alarm and the feeling that I'd overindulged.

It all changed again once I started walking down to the Bellevue under a milky sky. I noticed that my spirits were high. My plan not to stay more than half an hour yielded to the hope that I could eat lunch with Loos and be in his company again for as long as he was willing.

I sat down at our table on the terrace. It was almost eleven and Loos was nowhere to be seen. The windows of his room stood open, a sign that he was awake. I ordered a Campari. Loos was taking his time. I cleaned my spectacles. From time to time I looked up at the yellowish façade – nothing moved at the window. Maybe he had gone out for a walk. The waiter began to set the tables, a different one than the night before. After another half-hour I went into the restaurant; it was, after all, possible that Loos had forgotten where we were going to meet. He wasn't sitting there. When I got back to my table my glass had been taken away. The table was, unfortunately, reserved for twelve o'clock, the waiter said. 'For two people?' I asked. He nodded with irritation. I said I was one of them, so convinced was I that Loos had seen to it. 'Ah, I see,' said the waiter, and I sat down again and ordered another Campari. I looked up at Loos's window with growing impatience. At twelve the waiter came back followed by an elderly couple and asked what name the table had been reserved under. 'Loos,' I said, 'Mr Loos is a guest here at the hotel.' 'Just a moment,' said the waiter. He hurried off, came hurrying back again, and told me that there was nothing reserved under the name Loos. 'Strange,' I said. 'There must be a mis-understanding, I'm sorry.' I took my glass. To the side and up the stairs from the terrace, on the level of the entrance to the restaurant, there were two uncovered granite tables. I sat down at one in such a way that I could see both the entrance and the terrace. It got to be twelve-thirty. Loos had said he would be sitting on the terrace by eleven, as far as conditions allowed. I had assumed he meant the weather conditions. That was perhaps a mistake, I now realised. Maybe there were other reasons that prevented him from coming. At one it occurred to me that he might have left a message for me. I went to the reception desk. I gave my name and asked the woman there if there was a message for me from Thomas Loos, who was staying here. 'Loos?' she asked. She wrinkled her brow and reached for a book. 'We have no guest by that name,' she said. 'No, no, you do,' I said, 'we ate here twice, yesterday and the day before, in the evening.' The woman looked again in the guestbook and asked me whether I knew the room number. 'Not the number,' I said, 'but it's the room on the top floor on the far left, as you look from the terrace.' 'Uh-huh,' said the woman, taking a third look at the book. She then gave me a rather unfriendly look and said, 'I'm afraid I can't help you.' 'Listen,' I said, 'Mr Loos is my friend. We were going to meet here at eleven, but he didn't show up. I can't understand why you won't give me any information.' 'I can only tell you,' the woman said, 'that no guest with the name Loos is or has been staying with us and that the gentleman who was in the room you mentioned checked out early this morning.' 'A fairly large, heavy-set man with a strikingly deep voice?' I asked. She just shrugged her shoulders. I stared at her, flustered, and asked for his name. 'I'm sorry,' she said, 'we are obliged to confidentiality: customer protection.' 'Yes, but he's my friend,' I repeated, without realising in my confusion how little this statement was likely to help me. The woman only said that people normally knew their friends' names.

Normally, I thought in the car driving towards Agra, I am a person with a clear head and an analytic intelligence. At the moment I am no such person. At the moment my brain is in a tangle, and that's why I also forgot to pay for the two Camparis. I turned the car around and drove back to the Bellevue, where I paid the bill with trembling fingers.

At the house I took a long, cold shower till my overheated emotions cooled. The facts were essentially clear and their synopsis simple: Loos had stood me up. We had become close to each other; we had spent two long evenings in intensive conversation with each other, getting more personal by the hour; we had practically become friends – and nevertheless Loos had stood me up and disappeared without a goodbye. This was the one fact that cried out for an interpretation. But a second more egregious fact called out even louder: Loos – a cultivated, and seemingly respectable, if somewhat perverse, person – had been staying in a hotel under a false name.

I considered first whether I could have said something on the previous evening, something that rankled him to the point that he wanted to see no more of me. Nothing came to mind. There had been disagreements, of course, but that was no ground for feeling injured, and certainly no ground for a rupture. It seemed more probable that, like me, Loos had simply felt that he'd had enough in the morning, that he wanted to be alone and quiet, and had crept off somewhere where he could think about his dead wife undisturbed. But it also seemed possible that he took flight out of a mixture of embarrassment and disgruntlement. It often happens that a person who has confided in and revealed himself to someone is later embarrassed about it and feels an aversion to the person he's brought into his confidence. We don't always like people who know our secrets, and we can resent the fact that we have practically shown ourselves naked in front of them. And that sufficiently accounted for the first fact. The second was a harder nut to crack. What could have caused Loos to register under a false name? I looked first for the more innocent reasons. Maybe this sort of masquerade was just a whim. He might have found it fun or a release to shed his real name and go incognito, at least for a few days. I couldn't really imagine myself doing it, which of course means nothing – there are a lot of eccentricities that I have a hard time identifying with. But it was easier to believe in this interpretation than the more outlandish one that envisioned Loos on the run from the police, possibly even an escaped convict, who was driven by an inner compulsion to visit the vicinity of the crime, the place where his wife in some way or other – but by some act of his – had met her death.

Seized with a nervousness I'd never known before, I started pacing the house and garden. Suddenly I stopped. Suddenly it struck me: Loos had in fact stayed at the Bellevue for a few days last year. So they must already have known him – there was no way they could have forgotten such a striking man, or his name either. So how could Loos have dared to register under another, false name? That had to be excluded. But if I excluded that, only one conclusion remained – one that chilled me. It was I, then, I was the one who had been deceived. He had passed himself off to me as Loos, but his real name, in all probability, was the one in the guest book. I lay down on the sofa, but stood up again after a few minutes, because I can't think straight lying down. I was trying to figure out why the thing rattled me so much. Although it was a matter of deceit and deliberate misleading, I felt no moral indignation. That's not typical of me anyway. Besides, it was completely irrelevant to me whether Loos's real name was Meier or Müller; a false label doesn't change what it's attached to. But I was disappointed nonetheless, and I couldn't avoid asking myself: what can I believe that comes from a person who has made himself known to me under a false name and conversed with me for two long evenings? Doesn't the false label have to raise suspicions that he's told me other fairy tales? But I ruled this out: there wasn't the least ground for it. Only the story of his wife's death raised doubts, and only then, if I thought he was to blame or shared the blame for her death. Otherwise, everything I heard from Loos – I stay with this name for now – seemed credible.

I brooded over it a while longer, till I was forced to capitulate, to admit that I could find no answer to the central question. If it was after all true that Loos was not really named Loos, then what reason did he have to introduce himself to a complete stranger, an unknown – which I certainly was to him – under an assumed name? I could no longer accept a simple, whimsical mood as the explanation: my intuition spoke against it. My intuition said that Loos's name *was* Loos. What was an alias supposed to disguise? But there was no sudden flash of insight, and a growing inner tension, a restlessness I could hardly endure, obliterated what was left of my power to think.

I reached for the axe and chopped wood like a maniac till I was soaked with sweat and felt calmer. Then I took another cold shower, put fresh clothes on, and sat down behind the wheel of the car. As if by remote control – practically without my participation – it drove itself to Cademario.

I stood at the hotel bar and drank a double Fernet because my stomach was all in a knot. It was in this health resort that the decisive event played itself out, I said to myself. Where if not here will I learn the truth? Only why does it actually matter to me? Why should I care? I've never been curious in my life. Why the hell can't I manage to just slam the door on this whole thing, that has nothing to do with me? I only had to push myself, I had to rationally decide to let go of the matter, and I'd be free. So I pushed myself, finished my drink, and steered myself to the exit. But something pulled me left to the reception desk just before I got there. I asked whether Eva, a respiratory therapist – her last name had escaped me – still worked here at the sanatorium; I was an acquaintance of hers and would like to see her for a few minutes if I could. They asked me for my name, which I gave along with my title and was immediately told that Eva Nirak was off, since it was Pentecost, but was in the building somewhere, probably in her room. I waited in the big reception lobby and made a mental note not to blurt things out. I didn't want it to seem that I only came to ask her whether a fatal accident had occurred at the indoor pool a year ago. I wanted to chat with her for a while and then slip my question in somewhere as if in passing. She would have to know about it – she belonged to the staff. That she didn't say anything about it a year ago when we had our little roll in the hay meant nothing, since that afternoon we had naturally kept our talk to a minimum.

I hardly recognised Eva now when I saw her approach. Her loose platinum blonde hair was now chestnut brown and pinned up over her neck. She looked austere, almost bourgeois, and her grey suit strengthened this impression. Her eyes were cool, her lips unglossed and unsmiling, her handshake limp: I was clearly not welcome. Before I could say a word, she asked, 'Have you come because of me or because of her?' 'I don't know what you're talking about,' I said. 'You're too late,' she said, 'she left an hour ago.' 'But who, for God's sake?' 'Don't pretend. You found out somehow that Valerie spent the Pentecost holiday here. She's gone now, and I hardly think she wants to see you again. Leave her in peace!' 'Eva, I had no idea that Valerie was here. I don't even know where she lives now. I haven't heard another thing from or about her since last year, since we broke up.' 'Then you're here to see me, how flattering. Let's sit down.'

I followed her out to the panorama terrace feeling slightly dizzy. I ordered another Fernet, Eva a glass of red wine. 'Why did Valerie come here?' I asked her. 'To visit me, of course,' Eva responded. 'So you're still in touch, amazing,' I said. 'She's my friend.' 'But still, *then* you ... you know what I mean. Did you tell her?' 'There are things,'

Eva said, 'that are too meaningless to have to mention.' 'Thank you,' I said. 'Which doesn't mean,' she went on, 'that I wasn't surprised at myself then, at least afterwards. It shocked me that I could be like that.' 'We simply attracted each other,' I said. 'That can happen, don't be so austere. Did Valerie tell you about our separation, I mean before it happened?' 'Yes, she did, on the same day I was with you. What reason did *you* have for not telling me?' 'I probably thought it was a special turn-on for you to seduce a man in a relationship.' 'A sharp number like you,' said Eva, 'always sets our kind on fire, in a relationship or not.' 'It strikes me as a little strange when someone later casts a mocking light on the sharp number she was once so set on. I don't know how to account for your aggressiveness.' 'It has nothing to do with our little romp,' Eva said, 'but with Valerie.' 'You've going to have to be clearer,' I said. 'Did she say something bad about me?' 'Have you ever heard her say anything bad about other people?' 'Actually, no,' I said. 'She protected you,' Eva said. 'She took all the blame on herself for her misery.' 'Misery! Please. We had a beautiful time together, and when it ran its course, Valerie accepted it, with composure. She too clearly realised that we weren't suited to each other, not for the long run anyway.' 'Yes,' said Eva, 'you should have seen how serene she was the day after your visit. She didn't howl, she didn't tear her hair. Man, you don't have a clue. And I of all people – she didn't know anyone else here – I had to take her in my arms and console her, though I probably still smelled of you. You can imagine how shabby I felt.' 'I hope you're not making me responsible for that,' I said. 'If I'm not mistaken, you enjoyed your time with me on a totally voluntary basis.' 'That's true,' she said. 'At least I realised, thanks to you, how little the casual encounter suits me. It was a new experience for me, although I'm sure you believe the opposite.' 'You *radiated* the opposite.' 'Possibly so,' she said, 'but let's drop that. Are you really not aware of the desperate condition you left Valerie in?' 'I told you, she looked composed. She didn't shed a tear, and in the time since there hasn't been a single sign of desperation – no reproach, no lamentation, and no request to talk it out with me again either.' 'You've interpreted all of that in your own way,' said Eva, 'a way that's comfortable for you. The image of the silent Valerie, who calmly and without complaint goes on to the next item on the agenda, has spared you all empathy and all scruple.' 'I'm not a mind-reader,' I said indignantly. 'How can I know that someone's in pain if she doesn't show it in her face? And anyway, you're getting on my nerves. I have trouble with sermons.' 'You can leave anytime you want,' she said. 'Yes,' I said, 'that would be the smarter thing to do.' 'And yet it seems something is holding you back.' 'How do you get that?' 'Because you're constantly biting your lower lip and because I don't necessarily believe that you came here just to say hello to me.' 'Hmm,' I said, and Eva asked, 'Have you really heard nothing about Valerie?' 'Not the slightest thing.' 'She's moved far away and lives alone. She never got over the separation.'

We stayed quiet for a while. Then I said that, though I was convinced that Eva was exaggerating and trying to make me feel guilty, I was very sorry that Valerie had taken our separation so tragically. To hear that I meant so much to her was a surprise to me – she had never expressed anything like that. Apparently, said Eva, only what was said counted for me, to anything else I was blind. Valerie too was blind, of course, but in a different way. I said it was nevertheless a charming caprice of nature when two blind people found each other. Eva didn't take me up on that. A small misunderstanding, as she put it, had crept into our discussion: the separation Valerie hadn't been able to get over was the one from her husband, not from me. I swallowed dryly and asked Eva why, then, she had just now – and in dramatic tones to boot – reported on Valerie's pain and desolate condition after our separation. Because it had happened like that, she answered, because Valerie really was desperate. She had – and these were her exact words – loved me with a 'baffling ardour.' And yet she had always known that something in our relationship wasn't right. She had once told her, Eva, about a scene that she and I had witnessed at a children's playground. A child was sitting on the swing, while her father stood next to her, buried in a newspaper, mechanically giving the swing a push from time to time without lifting his head. I hadn't noticed how lovelessly lethargic and disengaged the father was. She, Valerie, overlooked this at the time, as with much else that she saw about me and turned a blind eye to. Her heart, with all her wits, seemed to have run off with her, is how Valerie had literally put it. She had enjoyed the whole process in a thoughtless way, and it very soon became clear to her that she couldn't impose herself on her husband in this state. And so she left him – although not with the feeling that it would be final – and suppressed her guilty feelings. Maybe I now had the impression, Eva continued, that Valerie had confided in her with everything having to do with me and her husband, but that wasn't the case. She had in truth told her very little, and very sparingly, as if she were trying to remember a dream. Especially with regard to her marriage with Felix – his name was surely known to me – she had spoken practically only in hints.

I knew what she was talking about, I said, she was like that with me too. She never came right out with anything, she preferred to keep things shrouded in mystery, which struck me more and more as an affectation and got on my nerves. It was a mistake, Eva observed, to draw conclusions about others based on ourselves. That much of my own behaviour was disingenuous didn't give me the right to interpret Valerie's behaviour in that sense and to talk about affectation. I asked Eva if she was taking psychology courses. She said she was sorry she couldn't help me there, but she would heartily recommend that I take one, although she didn't really think that empathy could be learned. In any case, she saw Valerie's behaviour and hesitant way of speaking primarily as a sign of her embarrassment and sense of tact. And to these were added her intuition and experience, which told her how infinitely difficult it was to get hold of something as contradictory as feelings with words. There was chaos reigning in Valerie – she had told Eva that herself – she felt both innocent and guilty, happy and oppressed, fulfilled and empty, and very often all simultaneously. And this was only an approximation of her real condition at the time. We really ought to be glad that she came out of it just with nervous problems instead of having a mental breakdown. I said I had caught on to her nervous condition, but that Valerie had explained it in a totally different way. There had been no talk of chaos in her feelings, and I had had so little sense of it that I found it rather difficult to give it any credence.

Eva sighed, the way people do when they want to let someone know that they find him tiresome and think it senseless to have any more to do with him. Nevertheless, I still asked – though it was actually more to finally bring the conversation around to Loos – whether Valerie had turned to me because of a crisis in her marriage. Eva said she didn't know, because Valerie hadn't given *her* much of a glimpse into the inner reality of her relationship either. She had put up a protective wall around the marriage, as it were, and she, Eva, had respected it and not tried to penetrate it. But if Valerie ever happened to casually speak of Felix, her tone became warmer, and you had the sense you could hear love behind it, so that it was completely unclear to her, Eva, why this woman was driven to throw herself into somebody else's arms. She could speculate, but didn't want to do that now. She could say with assurance, however, that neither a simple appetite for change nor the seductive arts of a skirt-chaser were the cause. I passed over the 'skirt-chaser' and said I thought it was a shame that the marriage didn't get back into shape. I had actually assumed and honestly hoped it would, wishing it for both their sakes. '"Noble be the man, helpful and good,"' said Eva. I passed unruffled over this remark too and added that, on the other hand, I could appreciate Felix's position. Not every man was capable of giving a warm welcome to an unfaithful wife when she came knocking at the door again. He had been capable of it, Eva said, he had received her with a virtual bouquet of roses. Did that mean, I asked, that Valerie didn't want to go back to him again? So it seemed, Eva said. On the other hand, unmistakable signs suggested that Valerie *did* want to go back to him, but wouldn't let herself. If that were the case, I said, then I'd be eager to know the reasons. They were filigree and hard to get at, Eva said. Did she know them then? I asked. She said she could feel them.

I let her feel them and ordered a mineral water. 'Did you ever meet him, I mean Felix Bendel?' I then asked. 'Not actually meet,' she said, 'but I saw him briefly by chance, back then, after his short visit to Valerie's room.' 'He visited her here?' 'That he did, at the end of her first week here. I remember, because she told me later.' 'Did he stay overnight?' 'Oh, the gentleman is jealous – who would have thought it! But I can reassure you. She was all too true to you, I should say "unfortunately".' 'All too true? What is that supposed to mean?' 'It means that Felix's last desperate attempt to win her back completely failed. She rejected him, for good, apparently. It must have been horrible for each of them. And when Valerie told me about it – in hints, as always – I realised immediately that it must have been Felix I met briefly in the elevator that evening. I was waiting on the ground floor, and when it came and I opened the door – it doesn't work automatically – there was a man facing me, looking pale, who stared at me with a haggard expression. I greeted him and stepped in, and since he had come down from an upper floor and wasn't getting out there, I assumed that like me he wanted the basement. But he didn't get out there either, so I asked him if he was looking for something particular. "The exit," he said in a hoarse voice. I said he had to go back up one floor, then go left along the corridor, and he'd come to the exit. That was my meeting with Bendel. But I see that it doesn't seem to interest you, you keep drumming with your fingers. So let's come out with it: why did you come here?'

I hadn't been conscious of the drumming, and I apologised for it and asked Eva without further ado whether the name Bettina Loos meant anything to her. She reflected, then shook her head and said, 'Never heard of her. Who is she?' 'Well, she was possibly a patient here at the same time as Valerie. You would have crossed paths with her.' Eva narrowed her eyes and gave me a searching look. 'Uh-huh,' she said, 'I get it. So you were active in three affairs! Did you think she'd be here? Or hope I could tell you where she is now?' 'Total nonsense,' I said, 'I had no relations with her. And she was here with her husband.' 'I sense that you're here about her.' 'That could be,' I said, 'but not the way you think. First of all, I've never met her, and secondly, she's dead.' 'It's beginning to dawn on me,' Eva said. 'You're a lawyer. Is this about a criminal case?' 'Maybe.' 'And why didn't you tell me right away what you wanted to see me for? You listen politely to stories about Valerie and you have something completely different on your mind.' 'Yes, no – I mean, I don't really know, Eva, I'm sorry. I'm a little confused, and I feel somehow ridiculous.' 'The first sympathetic thing you've said,' said Eva. 'So then, what's it about?'

'Let me say in advance that my interest is purely private – I'm not here as a lawyer. I'd just like to ask you whether there was an accident in June last year at the indoor pool here, and I mean one that resulted in death. The victim, a woman of about forty, is supposed to have slipped on the edge of the pool and died of her injuries hours later in a hospital in Lugano. Did you hear about it?' 'No,' said Eva, 'no, I know nothing of such an accident.' 'Could it be that it happened without coming to your attention?' 'That seems very unlikely to me. Certainly they would have handled it very discreetly; nevertheless something would have leaked out. Does this woman have something to do with the woman you mentioned – what's her name again?' 'Bettina Loos,' I said. 'Perhaps Bettina Loos, but perhaps that isn't her name.' 'How mysterious!' Eva said. 'It seems so,' I said, 'and yet a lot would be explained if you could find out two things: was a woman of this name a guest here last year? And second, did a woman, perhaps with another name, have an accident at the pool then, or otherwise die?' To my surprise, Eva said, 'You'll know both in five minutes. The director's here – I just saw him – he would know about the accident, and the computer will spit out the guest list from last June in three seconds. Be back soon.'

My stomach was still nervous, so I ordered another Fernet. I let my gaze wander over the Gulf of Agno to the Collina d'oro, which rose up a weak glaucous colour in the haze that wreathed it. Montagnola was only a blurred patch, and I cleaned my spectacles with impatient fingers. When Eva returned – her face betrayed nothing – she asked where I had got my information from. 'So it's right then?' I asked. 'It's not right,' she said. 'There was never a guest with the name Bettina Loos at this hotel, nor did a woman of any other name die of an accident here last June.' 'Not killed either? Or jumped from a balcony?' 'Not that either, Commissioner,' she said laughing. 'I checked everything. But on the other hand, I just now remembered that there was indeed an accident at the pool last June, though only a small one that turned out all right, as you know.' 'Don't play with my sanity! I don't have an inkling of what you're talking about!' 'You seem to be forgetting,' Eva said, 'didn't you meet a woman with a broken ring finger?' 'Ah, of course,' I said. 'But that didn't happen at the pool, it was in the woods. She didn't see a branch, or maybe it was a root, and tripped over it.' 'That's what she told people,' Eva said. 'It seemed less embarrassing to her than a slip on the edge of the pool.' 'Very strange,' I said. 'And because the finger swelled up,' Eva went on, 'the doctor had to clip the wedding ring off with a small pair of wire cutters. Did she mention that?' 'Of course not. She never wore a ring when we were together.' 'I can understand that,' Eva said. 'And now you owe me a *quid pro quo*. Where did you get that fairy tale, and what are you looking for here? What are you so intensely preoccupied with that you seem so completely immersed in it?'

'I met a man by chance at the Bellevue in Montagnola, a remarkable man, a little over fifty, a classical philologist. We became friends of a sort, talking with each other for two evenings. His name was Loos, Thomas Loos, physically a bear of a man. He had come down here, as he gradually revealed, to commemorate his wife, his dead Bettina, whom he revered like a saint – it came across as crazy to me. He was unquestionably disturbed, from time to time almost unbalanced – then completely normal again and impressively sharp-minded, especially when it came to proving how awful the present age is, how unbearable the world – the only thing he valued was his wife, his happy marriage. He seems to have placed her on a pedestal, and apparently more thoroughly so *after* her death than before. But the point is, he told me that after an operation – she had a brain tumour – she came to Cademario with him to recuperate, and then a couple days after that, the accident happened. She was brought to Lugano, the Ospedale Civico, where she died on the 11th of June. The rest can be stated in a few words. We agreed to meet this morning at the Bellevue, where he was staying, just to see each other quickly one more time. But he didn't show up, and when I asked for him, the woman at the reception desk said there was no hotel guest named Thomas Loos. I described where the room was situated. All she would say was that the gentleman had checked out and she was not allowed to tell me his name. At first I thought that he had registered under a false name, but I had good reason to abandon that notion, and concluded that this strange girl had lied to *me* and that his name wasn't Thomas Loos. The whole thing has roiled me up me so much that I drove over here in the hope of finding some clarity. Do you see now? What do you make of it?'

'I make nothing at all of it yet,' said Eva. 'I still know too little. Tell me more. What, for example, do two men talk about for two full evenings?' 'Well, first, as I hinted, the discussion was all "God and the world", but then we gradually got more personal, more intimate, you could say. For example, he asked me about my life as a bachelor and then along the way about my love life.' 'Did you tell him about Valerie?' 'That was the obvious choice, of course,' I said. 'It suggested itself once it came out that he and his wife were here at the spa at the same time briefly.' 'Which has since proved false beyond doubt,' said Eva. 'Was he very interested in your love life?' 'Not terribly,' I said, 'he listened politely enough, but yawned now and then too.' 'And Loos, what did he tell you about Bettina, I mean in detail – for example, outward appearance, or perhaps idiosyncrasies?' 'Different things,' I said. 'Why do you ask?' 'Woman's curiosity.' 'All right, then,' I said, 'he mentioned her blonde hair and her hourglass figure, and that she didn't eat meat, but loved raspberries. I can't remember right now – no, wait, she didn't smoke, and dancing didn't matter to her, and she loved a certain Schubert song about the beauty of the world, as well as – in contrast to Loos – Hesse's umbrella and one of his verses.'

'Listen, I'm getting cold,' Eva said, 'I'm going to go get a jacket. I'll be right back.'

She came back and was silent. She looked at me, not coolly – her look was gentle now, almost compassionate, regretful, as if to say, 'I'm sorry that I can't help you.' After a while I asked why she wasn't saying anything. Probably, she explained, because she was speechless. I said I could understand that, the whole thing was too bizarre. She found it extremely sad, she said and asked immediately if I knew what Felix did professionally. I said Valerie had told me he was a musician and gave cello lessons. 'I see,' said Eva. 'Why? Isn't it right?' I asked. 'In any case, he plays the cello,' she answered. 'You're really playing the Sybil,' I said. 'Thomas,' she said, 'I have to go now. I don't think I can help you. I'm only a respiratory therapist, the blind I can't heal.' 'Now what is that supposed to mean?' I asked. She asked back whether by any chance Loos had told me what the Hesse verse was about that his wife Bettina found so strikingly beautiful. 'Yes, roughly,' I said. 'Some piece of universal wisdom on the heart and parting.' 'Here,' said Eva and took a piece of squared notepaper, folded over, out of her jacket pocket. 'I give you this for the trip. Take care,' she said, got up, gave me her hand, and left me sitting there. I stuck the note in my pocket and stared mindlessly out into the landscape. Finally I called the waiter, paid, and left.

I stopped on the way, I don't remember where now, and took the note out of my pocket. I unfolded it and recognised Valerie's handwriting and then the two lines from Hesse:

And so the heart at every call from life
Must ready be to part and start anew.

Keep calm! I told myself, but my body wouldn't obey. I drove on in a state of distraction. A coincidence is far from being proof. How many women love Hesse? How many speak these lines, precisely these, from the heart, despite the embarrassingly artificial word order? Probably thousands! All right then. Bettina loved them, and Valerie too, apparently, although she kept them from me. Two women who like the same motto don't for that reason metamorphose into *one*. And Eva had put on airs, kept her ostensible knowledge to herself, to keep me on tenterhooks, and then handed me this note: apparently the only piece of evidence leading her to her absurd suspicion. No grounds for tenterhooks, I thought and then nevertheless – hardly back in Agra – knocked my freshly filled wine glass over.

I made a short call to the editor of the legal journal to tell him that, due to illness, I saw myself in no position to have my article ready by the deadline. Then I made a fire in the fireplace. I sat down in the chair in front of it and closed my eyes to collect myself.

For a few moments my sober nature seemed to take control again. I marvelled over the halfwit in me who had almost driven himself mad with wild speculation. I told myself that the further I entered into the labyrinth of improbabilities the more likely I was to lose the thread.

After the third glass of wine I fell to brooding again, and thus into vacillation. Words occurred to me, Loos's words, that all at once seemed suspect, ambiguous or sly. I tried to determine, with as much amused dispassion as I could muster, at what point he – if he was indeed Bendel – might have realised who was sitting across from him. At the latest, I thought, when I mentioned Valerie's name, maybe even earlier, when I mentioned that his wife and my girlfriend must have been at the spa at the same time. But as I clearly recalled, that hadn't really interested him. I thought of other junctures in the conversation that could have signalled my identity to him – and finally the one occasion that with a single stroke put a stop to all my hopping around. Right at the beginning I had introduced myself by name – Clarin, a name you don't hear every day, with the accent on the second syllable. Assuming that he knew of our affair and had once asked Valerie what this guy's name was, and assuming that she told him – then Loos, no, Bendel, would have had the picture from the outset. And therefore, then, the whole masquerade, the false name, and his outlandish webs of fabrication?

I only believed in this version of things for a short while, then I began to think that *I* was the one weaving webs. Would Bendel have befriended me? Would he have invented a tumour just for me? Would he have had Valerie die just to deceive me? That was all just too far-fetched. And then the lightning bolt in Hyde Park! Valerie would certainly have told me about such an unforgettable and unheard-of experience. And Bendel wouldn't have mentioned it, he would have betrayed himself in so doing. He would have to have assumed that I knew about it from her. But what if the lightning story was totally invented? Or simply plucked out of some newspaper? But what for? Loos might have been a bit unhinged from time to time, but mentally ill he was not.

I cooked up some noodles and fried a couple of eggs, which I ate distractedly and without pleasure. And back at the fireplace, the speculations started again, the brooding, the unbearable back-and-forth. I started feeling dizzy, and the flickering of the flames, which I usually found soothing, only made it worse. I stared into the fire and saw there the image of Loos, how he had stared into the flames. And then for the first time it struck me that if *Bendel* had sat here, then I was assured of his hatred, and I had a deadly enemy.

I commanded myself to pull myself together. I had to do something to quell the turmoil in me, to unravel the threads and take stock of myself. I wasn't really looking for certitude at that moment, just order and an overview.

I went into the next room and sat in front of the laptop. I heard knocking, and my heart immediately started knocking too. I felt: Loos is here, Loos has come to explain why he wasn't there this morning, he's come to say goodbye. I opened the front door: there was no one to be seen. I seemed to be hearing things. The floorboards get warped sometimes and then make a cracking sound.

I shut the door and sat down again. Then I typed two sentences: 'Everything's turning. And everything's turning round him.' I couldn't go further. I couldn't peck what was plaguing me out onto the keys. I walked around in the room. The photograph of Tasso on the bookshelf reminded me of his fountain pen, that Magdalena had given me as a memento. Of course, I thought and took it, with the bottle of ink, from the lowest drawer of the desk. It smelled a little the way my grandmother sometimes smelled, of camphor, I think. I cleaned its inner parts and the reservoir with water and filled it with the old blue ink. When I began to write, it very quickly took on the temperature of my hand.